THE LAKE

Yasunari Kawabata

Translated by
Reiko Tsukimura

KODANSHA INTERNATIONAL
Tokyo • New York • London

Distributed in the United States by Kodansha America, Inc., 114 Fifth Avenue, New York, N.Y. 10011.

Published by Kodansha International Ltd., 17-14 Otowa 1-chome, Bunkyo-ku, Tokyo 112, and Kodansha America, Inc. Copyright © 1974 by Hideko Kawabata. All rights reserved. Printed in Japan.

LCC 73-89699
ISBN 0-87011-365-8
ISBN 4-7700-0697-7 (in Japan)

First edition, 1974
First paperback edition, 1978
93 94 95 15 14 13 12

Gimpei Momoi arrived in Karuizawa at the end of the summer season, although up there it seemed more like autumn. He bought a pair of flannel slacks and changed out of his old ones. He had on a new sweater and a new shirt, and since the night air was cold and foggy, he also bought a blue raincoat. Karuizawa was a good place for ready-made clothes. He even bought some comfortable shoes and left his old pair in the shoe store. But what was he to do with his old clothes, which he had wrapped in a piece of cloth? If he threw them into some empty house, they would not be discovered until the following summer. Turning into an alley, he felt with his hands along the window of a deserted villa, but it was boarded up with wood and nails. He did not want to break the window; after all, that was illegal.

Gimpei wondered whether he was really a wanted criminal, since his crime might not have been reported by the victim. He stuffed the clothes into a trash box and felt relieved. As he pressed the bundle down he could hear the sound of damp paper. Perhaps the vacationers were untidy or the caretaker was lazy,

5

for the box had not been emptied and the lid wouldn't close tightly. But it did not bother him.

After he had gone about thirty paces he turned around. He thought he saw a swarm of silver moths fluttering up into the mist near the trash box. When he stopped and was on the point of retracing his steps, the silvery vision passed overhead, throwing a dim, bluish light across the larch trees above him, and vanished. The trees stood in a row as on an avenue, at the end of which was an arched gateway decorated with ornamental lights. It was the entrance to a Turkish bath.

As he entered the garden, Gimpei ran a hand over his head. His hair seemed to be in good shape. In fact, people were often surprised by the skill with which he cut his own hair with a razor blade.

An attendant—one of the most popular there—led him to the bathroom. After closing the door, she took off her white jacket. She wore only a bra above the waist.

When she started to unbutton his raincoat, Gimpei involuntarily pulled away, but finally allowed himself to be undressed. Kneeling at his feet, she tugged off his socks.

Gimpei climbed into the perfumed bath. The color of the tiles made the water look green. The perfume was not very pleasant, but after his furtive moves from one cheap hotel to another in Shinano it smelled of flowers. When he got out of the bath, the woman

6

washed him all over. Squatting down at his feet she even washed in between his toes with her girlish fingers. He looked down at her head. Her hair was cut to a little below the nape of the neck and hung straight and loose, in the intimate way women left their hair after washing it.

"Shall I wash your hair?"

"What? Do you even wash your customers' hair?"

"Yes, I'll wash it for you."

Gimpei shrank back at the sudden thought of how his hair must smell. It had not been washed for a long time, and only trimmed with a razor blade. But as his hair was rubbed into a soapy lather, Gimpei, with his head bent forward and his elbows resting on his knees, felt his timidity disappear.

"You have a lovely voice, you know."

"Voice?"

"Yes. It lingers on even after you've stopped speaking. I wish it would go on forever. It feels as though something gentle and delicate were sinking through my inner ear into the core of my brain. Really, it would make even the most hardened criminal as meek as a lamb."

"Oh? I'm sure it's dreadfully coy and girlish."

"Not coy. It's incredibly sweet. It's got something sad and something tender, and at the same time it's fresh and open. It's different from a singer's voice. Are you in love?"

7

"No. It would be nice if I were."

"Wait. When you say something, don't scrub my head so hard. I can't hear your voice very well."

The girl stopped.

"You make me too shy to speak," she said, embarrassed.

"I never thought I'd ever meet anyone whose voice could sound so like an angel's. Even if I heard you say a few words over the phone I'd be listening for that lingering echo."

Gimpei was almost moved to tears. Her voice had aroused in him a sense of pure happiness and warm relief. Was this the voice of the eternal woman, or the compassionate mother?

"Where do you come from?"

The girl did not answer.

"From heaven?"

"Oh, no. From Niigata."

"Niigata?... Niigata City?"

"No. It's a small town."

The bath girl's voice, now low and soft, trembled slightly.

"Ah, the snow country... That's why your skin is so clear and beautiful."

"No. It's not beautiful."

"Yes, it is. But your voice is something special."

When she had finished scrubbing his hair, she poured several bucketfuls of hot water over it, wrapped a large towel around his head and rubbed it dry. She ran a comb through it a few times.

Then Gimpei, with a big towel around his waist, was put into the steam bath. The girl opened the front panel of the square wooden box and gently pushed him in. A board on top of the box had a place for his head to fit in, and once it was settled in snugly, she brought down a lid which shut off the remaining space.

"A guillotine," he said instinctively, and his wide eyes stared round in fright. Trapped in the hole, he turned his head to left and right. But the girl didn't notice his fear.

"Customers often say so," she said.

His glance shifted from the door to the window.

"Shall I close the window?" The girl was walking toward it.

"No."

The window was open, perhaps because the hot air of the steam bath filled the room. The light from the bathroom shone on the green leaves of the elm tree outside. The elm was large, and the light could not penetrate far into its dense foliage. Gimpei thought he heard the faint sound of a piano filtering through the darkness of the leaves, but the sound made no music. He must be hallucinating.

"Is there a garden outside the window?"

"Yes."

Half-naked against the window, lit dimly with a

greenish light, the fair-skinned girl seemed part of another world. Her feet were bare against the pale pink, tiled floor. Her legs were certainly youthful, but there were dark marks in the hollows behind her knees.

Gimpei was thinking that if he were left alone in the bathroom he would find it unbearable; he would panic, afraid that the rim of the slot would tighten its hold and strangle him. From under his seat he could feel the heat rising. His back leaned against what seemed to be a hot board. In fact, three sides of the box were hot from the steam.

"How long am I supposed to stay here?"

"That's up to you, but I think about ten minutes. Regular customers spend about fifteen minutes in it."

He looked at the small clock on the clothes locker near the door. Only four or five minutes had passed. The girl came to place a cold, damp towel on his forehead.

"I see. This makes the blood come to one's head."

Feeling relaxed, he could now imagine how silly he must look with only his solemn face sticking out of the wooden box. He tried to rub his warm chest and belly. His body was sticky, but he was not sure whether the moisture was perspiration or steam. He closed his eyes.

There was a splashing sound as the girl, apparently needing something to do while her customer was in the steam bath, baled hot water out of the perfumed bath and washed the floor. To Gimpei it sounded like waves beating against a rock. On the rock two seagulls with arched wings were pecking at each other's beaks. The sea of his native village appeared before his eyes.

"How many minutes now?"

"About seven."

Again the girl brought a damp towel and placed it on Gimpei's forehead. At the sudden, pleasurable cold he jerked his head forward.

"Ouch!"

"What's wrong, sir?"

Probably imagining that Gimpei was dizzy from the heat of the steam, the girl retrieved the towel he had let drop and returned it to his forehead, holding it there with her hand.

"Do you want to get out now?"

"No. There's nothing wrong."

Gimpei was seized by a fantasy. He was chasing this girl with the sweet voice along a street where streetcars ran, somewhere in Tokyo. For a while he saw only the ginkgo trees that lined the sidewalk. He was drenched in sweat. Realizing that he was unable to turn around since his head was pilloried in the wooden box, he screwed up his face in discomfort.

The girl left his side. She seemed a little wary of his behavior.

"About how old do I look with only my head

sticking out?" he asked, but the girl was confused and did not know how to answer.

"I can't tell men's ages."

The girl did not bother to look at him closely. He had no reason to tell her that he was thirty-four. She must still be under twenty, he thought. Her shoulders, belly and legs suggested she was still a virgin. Her cheeks were fresh and rosy, with only a trace of rouge on them.

"I'd like to get out now."

Gimpei's voice was mournful. The girl opened the board in front of his throat. Holding the two ends of the towel that was slung around his neck, she gently drew his head out as though it were some precious object. Then she wiped off the sweat which covered his body. He had a large towel wrapped around his waist. The girl spread a white sheet over a couch along the wall and made him lie face down on it. She started to massage him, working from the shoulders.

Gimpei hadn't realized that a massage was not just stroking and rubbing, but also tapping and patting with open hands. The attendant's palms were still a girl's, but the slaps on his back were continuous and surprisingly strong, and it made his breath come out in short gasps. He remembered his own child slapping him on the forehead with all the force in its round palm and continuing to beat him on the head when he lowered his face. When had that been?... But the hands of the little child were now beating wildly at the bottom of a grave against the wall of earth that weighed down on it. From all directions the dark walls of a prison closed in on Gimpei. He broke out in a cold sweat.

"Are you putting on powder?" he asked.

"Yes. Do you feel uncomfortable?"

"Oh no," Gimpei said hastily, "I'm already sweating again, aren't I? You know, it would be almost a crime to feel uncomfortable listening to your voice."

The girl suddenly stopped working.

"When I hear your voice, everything else disappears. I know it sounds a bit farfetched, but a voice can't be chased or caught, can it? I suppose it's like the flow of time or life. No, it needn't be. You can use your lovely voice whenever you want, but when you choose to be silent as you are now, nobody can make you produce it. Of course you can be made to speak out suddenly in surprise or anger or grief, but you're free to choose whether or not to talk in your natural voice."

The bath girl, silent in that freedom, continued to massage Gimpei's hips and the back of his thighs. She stroked the arch of his foot down to his toes.

"Would you like to lie on your back?" The girl spoke in such a low voice that it was scarcely audible.

"What?"

"This time, lie face up, will you?"

"Up? You want me to lie on my back, do you?"

13

Gimpei turned, holding the towel wrapped around his waist. Like the fragrance of flowers, the girl's low whisper, which came with the faintest suggestion of a shudder, filled his ears and followed him as he moved his body. He had never felt this sweet ecstasy before in his ears.

Standing with her body pressed against the narrow couch, the girl rubbed Gimpei's arms. Her breasts were above his face. Though her bra did not seem to be very tightly fastened, her flesh was slightly constricted along the edge of the white cloth. The way her breasts were set off from her body, however, showed that they had not yet developed into full maturity. She had rather a classical, oval face. Her forehead was not broad, but perhaps because her hair was pulled straight back and not fluffed out, it looked high and made her wide eyes even brighter. The flesh between her neck and shoulders was not full, and her upper arms were youthful and round. The sheen of her skin was so close to him that Gimpei shut his eyes. Behind his eyelids he saw a box, like a carpenter's nail box, full of tiny nails all glinting in the light. Gimpei opened his eyes and looked up at the ceiling. It was white.

"Don't you think my body looks old for my age? It's because I've had a hard life," Gimpei muttered. But he still hadn't told her his age.

"I'm thirty-four, you know."

"Are you? You look younger," the girl said, sup-

14

pressing any expression in her voice. She had moved round to stand at Gimpei's head and was rubbing the arm that lay next to the wall.

"My toes are long, aren't they?—just like a monkey's. They look shriveled, though in fact I walk quite a lot... I'm always horrified when I look at my toes. But you touched them with your beautiful hands. Weren't you shocked when you took off my socks?"

The girl did not answer.

"I come from the Japan Sea coast, too. It's rugged there, with black rocks. I used to walk barefoot, clinging to the rocks with my long toes."

Gimpei told half-truths. How many times in his youth had he told different lies because of his ugly feet? But it was true that even the skin of his insteps was dark and coarse, his arches were wrinkled, and the long, crooked toes could bend to any shape. Lying on his back as she massaged him, he could not see his feet, so he held up his hands above his face to inspect them. The girl was massaging the muscle from his chest to his arm, somewhere above his breast. Gimpei's hands did not seem as odd as his feet.

"Which part of the Japan Sea coast?" the girl asked in a natural voice.

"The part..." Gimpei mumbled. "I don't like talking about the place where I was born. I'm different. I haven't got a home any more."

15

The girl didn't seem particularly interested in knowing about Gimpei's hometown and was not listening with any special attention. How was the bathroom lit? There seemed to be no shadows on her body. While massaging his chest, she pushed her breasts forward and he closed his eyes, not knowing where to put his hands. If he stretched his arms along his body he might touch her. He thought he would be slapped on the face if so much as a fingertip brushed against her. And he could actually feel the shock of being slapped. In sudden terror he tried to open his eyes, but his eyelids refused to move. They had been hit very hard. He thought he might cry, but no tears came, and his eyes ached as though they had been pricked with a hot needle.

It was not the girl's palm but a blue leather handbag that had hit Gimpei's face. He hadn't known at the time that it was a handbag, but after feeling the blow he found a bag lying at his feet. He wasn't certain whether it had been used to strike him or had been thrown at him. What was certain was that he had been hit, because at that moment he came to his senses.

Gimpei had cried out, then started calling after the woman to stop. His immediate reaction was to tell her she had dropped her handbag. But the woman's back disappeared as she turned the corner of a drugstore. Only the blue handbag remained in the center of the road as if to offer tangible evidence of his crime. A bundle of one-thousand-yen bills jutted out between the open clasps of the bag. But it was the handbag, which might become evidence of a crime, that first attracted his attention and not the bundle of money. By running away and leaving the handbag behind, the woman seemed to have turned his action into a crime. Frightened, he automatically reached for the bag. It was after he had picked it up that he saw, to his astonishment, the bundle of one-thousand-yen bills.

Later, he wondered if the drugstore itself had not been a hallucination. It was strange to find a small, old drugstore in the residential area when no shops were expected there at all. Beside the glass doors, however, he had seen a signboard advertising a medicine for tapeworm. And strangely enough, there had been two almost identical fruit stores facing each other on the corner across the streetcar tracks where the residential area began. In both stores there were small wooden boxes of cherries and strawberries on display. While he was following the woman, Gimpei saw nothing except her. Then why, all of a sudden, had the two fruit stores caught his eye? Had he wanted to remember the corner because it pointed the way to the woman's house? The fruit stores must really have been there for, even now, the appearance of the strawberries, neatly laid out in their boxes, lingered before his eyes. Yet there might have been only one store on the corner of the road where the streetcars ran, and in the confusion of the moment he could have persuaded himself that there were fruit stores on both sides. Later, he had had to fight hard against the temptation to return and find out whether the fruit stores and the drugstore really existed. But in point of fact, even the street itself was hard to recall, and he could only get a vague idea of it by drawing a map of Tokyo in his head. For at the time, all that had mattered was which way the woman had gone.

"Right. She might not have intended to throw it away," Gimpei muttered involuntarily while his stomach was being massaged by the girl.

Startled, he opened his eyes wide, but closed them again before the girl could notice. Their expression might have reminded her of some ghostly bird of hell. He had mumbled something about a woman's handbag, but fortunately he hadn't revealed either the object thrown away or the person who had thrown it. He felt his abdomen suddenly contract and heave.

"It's tickling," Gimpei said as an excuse, and the girl worked more slowly. Now he really felt he was being tickled. He burst into genuine laughter.

Until that precise moment, Gimpei's interpretation had been that, whether she had in fact hit him with the bag or thrown it at him, the woman had thought he was following her for the money it contained—a fear which, reaching the point of hysteria, made her abandon the bag and flee. But she might not have intended to throw her bag away. She might in fact have tried to knock him aside with what she was carrying, but the force of her action carried the handbag out of her hands. Whatever had happened, Gimpei and the woman must have been very close to each other for the bag to have hit him in the face the moment she swung it. As they entered the lonely residential district, it could be that, without realizing, he had shortened the distance at which he followed her. Had the woman noticed his approach and run away, hurling her bag at him?

Robbery had not been his motive. He had not remotely suspected, or even bothered to consider, that the bag had contained such a large amount of money. When he picked up the handbag, intending to remove such obviously incriminating evidence, he had found two hundred thousand yen inside. Since there were two bundles of crisp bank notes, each for one hundred thousand yen, and also a passbook, the woman could have been on her way from the bank. She might have thought that she had been followed from there. Apart from the two bundles of bank notes, the bag only contained about sixteen hundred yen in cash. Opening the passbook, he saw that twenty-seven thousand yen or so remained after the woman had withdrawn the two hundred thousand. She had withdrawn most of her savings.

Gimpei learned from the passbook that the woman's name was Miyako Mizuki. If he had had no intention of taking the money and had only been lured on by her strange appeal, he ought surely to have sent the money and passbook back to her. But as it was, he couldn't be expected to return them. Just as he had followed the woman, so the money followed him, like a living being with a mind of its own. It was the first time Gimpei had stolen money. Or rather, not that he had stolen it, but that the money had intimidated him, refusing to go away.

When he picked up the handbag, nothing had been farther from his mind than stealing the money. He realized that he was holding the evidence of a crime and, stuffing the bag under his jacket, he hurried out into the road where the streetcars ran. It was a pity it was not the season for overcoats. He plunged into a nearby store, bought a square piece of cloth and ran off with the handbag wrapped up in it.

Gimpei had been living alone in a rented upstairs room. He burned the passbook in his small, clay brazier, as well as a handkerchief and some other things belonging to Miyako Mizuki. As he had not made a note of the address shown on her passbook, it was lost forever. He no longer even contemplated returning the money. The burning passbook, handkerchief, and comb gave off a strong smell. Since the leather handbag would have smelled even worse if he had burned it,

Gimpei cut it into small pieces and spent the following days feeding one piece at a time into the fire. The non-combustible objects such as the clasp, the lipstick and the metal parts of the compact he threw into a ditch at midnight. Even if someone chanced to discover them, they would be too ordinary to attract attention. His hands trembled as he pushed up what little was left of the lipstick.

Gimpei listened carefully to the radio and read the papers closely, but he found no news about the robbery of a handbag containing two hundred thousand yen and a passbook.

"Mmm. . . As I thought, she hasn't reported it after all. There must be something that prevented her from doing so," Gimpei muttered to himself and felt the dark depths of his heart lit suddenly by a lurid flame. Perhaps he had followed the woman because something inside her made her susceptible to being chased by him. They might be inhabitants of the same infernal world. He could see it from his own experience. He rejoiced at the thought that Miyako Mizuki might be like him, and bitterly regretted not having copied down her address.

Miyako must certainly have been frightened while she was being followed by Gimpei, but she might also have experienced a tingling pleasure, without recognizing its presence. Can an entirely one-sided pleasure really exist in the human world? Had it not, perhaps, been like a drug addict's sensing out a fellow sufferer, that he should have made a special point of following Miyako when there were so many other pretty women walking about town?

Hisako Tamaki, the first woman he had ever followed, had clearly been a case of this sort. At the time she had been merely a young girl, younger even than the sweet-voiced bath attendant. Hisako had been a high-school student and Gimpei's pupil, and when his relationship with her was discovered, he was dismissed from his teaching post.

Gimpei had followed her until he reached the outer entrance of her house, but he had stopped there, taken aback by the grandeur of the portal. The gate, hinged to the stone wall and decorated with an arabesque design above the iron bars, stood open. Hisako turned back to look at him through the grillework.

"Sir," Hisako called to Gimpei. Her pale face began to flush beautifully. He also felt his own cheeks burning.

"Oh, is this your house, Miss Tamaki?" Gimpei said in a hoarse voice.

"What do you want, sir? Have you come to visit us?"

There could be no simple explanation why a teacher should follow his pupil secretly in order to visit her home. But Gimpei looked over the gate as if admiring the house and said:

22

"Yes. I'm glad a house like this wasn't burned down during the war. It's a miracle."

"Our house was burned down. We bought this one after the war."

"After the war?. . . What does your father do, Miss Tamaki?"

"Do you have any business here, sir?" Hisako said from the other side of the grillework, staring at Gimpei with angry eyes.

"Oh, yes. It's athlete's foot, actually. . . You see, Miss Tamaki, your father knows a good medicine for athlete's foot, doesn't he?" As Gimpei spoke, he wondered why he had had to mention this skin disease in front of such a magnificent gate, and he screwed up his face as though on the verge of tears. Hisako's clear, level look, however, never wavered.

"Athlete's foot?"

"Yes, a medicine for athlete's foot. Don't you remember you were talking to your friend at school about a medicine that was good for it?"

Her eyes told him she was trying to remember.

"It's so bad that I can't walk any more. Would you be good enough to go and ask your father the name of that medicine? I'll wait here."

When he was sure she had disappeared into the entrance of the Western-style house, Gimpei started to run. He felt pursued by his own hideous feet.

He did not think Hisako would report him either to

her family or to the school, but he was tortured by a severe headache, his eyelid twitched, and he had difficulty falling asleep that night. When he finally dropped off, his light rest was often broken. Each time he woke up he put his hands to his clammy forehead, and a headache would start again whenever the poison at the back of his head moved up over his crown to his forehead.

His headaches had begun while he was wandering through a nearby amusement quarter after his flight from the gate of Hisako's house. Unable to stand, Gimpei had crouched in the middle of the crowded street, holding his head in his hands. Along with the headache, he was overcome with dizziness. It seemed as if the bell that announced the winning ticket in a lottery were jangling in his head. The bell also reminded him of a fire engine racing along.

"What's wrong with you?" A woman's kneecap brushed Gimpei lightly on the shoulder. When he turned round to look up, he thought she was one of those streetgirls who frequented the postwar amusement quarter.

Still feeling unwell, Gimpei painfully dragged himself up against the shopwindow of a florist's and out of the way of passers-by. His forehead pressed against the glass of the shopwindow.

"You've been following me, haven't you?" Gimpei said to the woman.

"I don't think I was following you exactly."

"I don't suppose I was following you, was I?"

"Sure."

The woman's answer was ambiguous. If it had been affirmative she might have added something. But she paused, and Gimpei growing impatient said:

"If I wasn't doing the chasing, then it must have been you."

"Whichever it was, does it matter?..."

The woman's figure was reflected in the window. She seemed to be standing among the flowers beyond the glass.

"Whatever are you doing? Stand up quickly. People are staring at you. Is something the matter?"

"Yes. I've got athlete's foot."

Gimpei was surprised at himself when these same words came to his lips.

"It hurts so much I can't walk."

"You're disgusting. I know a nice place around here where we can go and relax. You ought to take off your socks and shoes."

"I don't want other people to look at them."

"I won't look at them. Not your feet, at any rate..."

"You'll catch it, mind you."

"It can't be catching." The woman put her hand under his arm and yanked him up. "Come on, now."

Still clasping his forehead in his left hand, Gimpei was watching her face reflected in the flowers when another woman's face appeared amid the flowers beyond the glass. Gimpei wondered if this was the owner of the flower shop. As though reaching out to seize a bunch of white dahlias on the other side of the window, he thrust his right hand against the glass and stood up. The proprietress of the shop glared at him from beneath thin, knitted eyebrows. Afraid that he might plunge his arm through the big glass window and cut himself, he shifted his weight toward the woman. She managed to keep her balance.

"Don't run away, now! Okay?" she said and suddenly pinched him sharply on the chest.

"Ouch!"

Gimpei felt revived. He hadn't understood clearly why he had come to the amusement quarter after fleeing from Hisako's house, but the moment this woman pinched him his head cleared. He felt refreshed, as if a breeze from the mountain by the lake had passed over him. It must have been the cool breeze of late spring, yet an ice-covered lake appeared before his eyes—perhaps because he had been afraid his arm might crash through the florist's window, which was as broad as a lake. It was the lake by his mother's village. There was also a town on the lakeshore, but his mother's home was in the village.

The lake lay in a shroud of mist, and all beyond the ice near the shore looked infinitely remote. Gimpei had tricked his cousin Yayoi into trying to walk on the ice, for as a boy he had borne a grudge against Yayoi and cursed her. His sinister hope was that the ice under her feet would give way and that she would sink into the water. Yayoi was two years older than Gimpei, but he was more cunning. When he was ten his father had met a strange death, and disturbed by the fear that his mother might leave him and return to her own family, Gimpei had had more need than Yayoi to develop a cunning streak in his character. Yayoi, on the other hand, made one feel that she had been brought up in the warmth of the spring sun. Among other reasons, it was perhaps this hidden desire not to lose his mother that had led him to his first love, this cousin on his mother's side. As a boy, it had been his greatest joy to walk with Yayoi along the shore of the lake, watching their reflection linked in the water beside them. As he walked and looked down at the lake, he felt that their figures would move together on the water forever.

But his happiness did not last. By the time she was fourteen or fifteen the girl seemed to have forgotten Gimpei; she was two years older and had discovered that he belonged to the opposite sex. And after the death of his father his mother's family came to dislike his father's relatives. Yayoi treated him coldly and was openly contemptuous. It was at about this time that he had wanted the ice on the lake to break and Yayoi to sink beneath it. Later, Yayoi married a naval officer,

27

and Gimpei heard that she had been left a widow.

It was the plate glass in the flower shop that had reminded Gimpei of the ice on the lake.

"How dare you pinch me," Gimpei said to the woman, rubbing his chest. "I'm sure you've given me a bruise."

"Ask your wife to look at it when you get home."

"I haven't got a wife."

"That's a likely story!"

"No, honestly. I'm a bachelor schoolteacher," Gimpei said calmly.

"And I'm a single schoolgirl," the woman replied.

Knowing she was talking nonsense, he had not even bothered to look into her face, but when he heard her say "schoolgirl" his headache started again.

"Is that infection hurting you? I said you'd better not walk too much. . ." The woman looked at his feet.

Gimpei wondered what Hisako would have thought had she been following him—just as he had followed her to the gate of her house—and had found him with this sort of woman. He stared quickly round at the crowd. Even if Hisako had not returned to the gate after disappearing through the front door, he was convinced at least that she was still following him in her heart.

The next day Gimpei took Hisako's class for Japanese. Hisako was waiting outside the classroom door.

"Sir, the medicine," she said as she hurriedly slipped something into his pocket.

He hadn't prepared for the class owing to his headache and, tired by a sleepless night, he gave the students some writing to do. He said they could choose their own subjects. One boy raised his hand.

"Sir, could I write about a disease?"

"Yes. Anything at all."

"For instance . . . sorry to mention such a filthy subject . . . but even athlete's foot?"

There was a sudden, loud burst of laughter. But everyone was looking at the boy, and no one even glanced with any curiosity at Gimpei. They were apparently laughing at the boy and not at him.

"Even that will do, I suppose. It's just possible I might find it informative, as I don't know anything about it," Gimpei said and glanced at Hisako's desk. The students laughed again, but it was laughter that sided with him in his innocence. Writing with her head lowered, Hisako did not look up. But her ears had turned red.

When Hisako brought her essay to his desk, Gimpei saw that its title was "Impressions of My Teacher." He thought it must be about himself.

"Miss Tamaki, stay behind after class, please," Gimpei said to Hisako. With only the faintest sign of assent, she raised her eyes and stared at him. He felt he was being glared at.

29

Walking over to the window, Hisako gazed out at the playground for a time.

When all the students had handed in their essays, she turned back and came up to his desk. After he had slowly put the essays in order, Gimpei stood up. He said nothing until he was out in the hall. Hisako was following about a yard behind.

"Thank you for the medicine." Gimpei turned around. "Did you speak to anyone about my athlete's foot?"

"No."

"You didn't speak to anybody?"

"No. But I told Miss Onda. She's my best friend."

"Miss Onda. Did you?..."

"Only Miss Onda."

"Once you've told one person, it's the same as telling everybody."

"No, it's not. It's only between Miss Onda and me. We've promised to tell each other everything."

"You're that close, are you?"

"Yes. You learned about my father's skin trouble when you heard me talking about it with Miss Onda."

"Did I? So you don't keep any secrets from Miss Onda? Well, it's just not true. Think carefully. Even if you were together day and night and told her everything that came into your head, it would still be impossible to tell her *everything*. Suppose, for example, that you have a dream one night and forget it

30

the next morning. Then you can't tell that to Miss Onda. It might even be a dream about breaking up with her and wanting to kill her."

"I don't have dreams like that."

"Anyway, it's just a morbid fantasy, a cover for girlish weaknesses, to believe in the kind of intimate friendship where you share absolutely everything. Perfect awareness might exist in heaven or hell, but not in the human world. If you have no secrets from Miss Onda it means that you don't exist, that you're not living your own life. Be completely honest with yourself and think about what I'm saying."

Hisako seemed unable to grasp either Gimpei's reasoning or why he was talking to her in this way.

"Why shouldn't I believe in friendship?" she protested finally.

"Friendship is impossible without secrets. Not only friendship, but no other human emotion can survive without them."

"What?" The girl still seemed unable to understand. "I talk to Miss Onda about everything important."

"I wonder. . . I can hardly believe you talk about the most important things of all, or the most unimportant, for that matter—the grains of sand on the seashore. I wonder what importance you attach to the skin disease your father and I have? You probably put that somewhere in the middle, don't you?"

31

Gimpei's words were so spiteful that Hisako felt as if she had been suddenly dropped after dangling in midair. She turned pale and seemed on the verge of tears. Gimpei continued in a gentle, coaxing voice.

"Do you tell Onda about everything that happens even in your family? I don't suppose you do. You don't tell her the secrets of your father's business, do you? Of course not, you see. Incidentally, I imagine you've written about me in your essay today. But there are things in the essay that you haven't told Onda, aren't there?"

Hisako looked at Gimpei with her tearful, piercing eyes. She remained silent.

"I don't know what business your father has turned into such a huge success since the end of the war. But, though I'm not Onda, I'd like you to tell me about it sometime—in detail."

Gimpei sounded casual, but his words were meant as an obvious threat. If her father had bought that house since the war, then it was natural to suspect him of having done something criminal or illegal such as dealing on the black market. Gimpei deliberately mentioned her father in the hope of making her keep quiet about the way he had followed her.

At the same time Gimpei reminded himself of what he had thought the previous evening: that Hisako would not report him. In spite of what had happened he had no reason to worry since she had come to his class that day, had given him the medicine for athlete's foot and had written an essay entitled "Impressions of My Teacher."

It was possible that Gimpei had followed Hisako in an unconscious way, as though drunk or sleepwalking, lured on by her charms. She had already cast a spell over him. Moreover, the very fact that she had been followed the day before could have made Hisako aware of her power of attraction and awakened in her, too, a secret thrill of pleasure. In any case, he felt intensely stirred by this intriguing, mysterious girl.

When Gimpei looked up after his threatening remark to Hisako, thinking that matters had now been settled, he found Nobuko Onda standing at the end of the hall watching them.

"Your friend's worried. She's waiting for you. Look." Gimpei let Hisako go. She did not run off to meet Onda as most girls would, but slowly dropped behind, apparently walking with her head down.

Three or four days later Gimpei thanked Hisako.

"That medicine—it's great, isn't it? Thank you. I'm completely cured now."

"Oh, really?" Hisako blushed beautifully, and lovely dimples appeared in her cheeks.

But she did not remain long the shy, lovely Hisako she had first been. Instead her relationship with Gimpei developed to the point where Onda reported him and he was ultimately dismissed from the school

While the bath attendant massaged his belly at the Turkish bath in Karuizawa, Gimpei, after all these years, could still imagine Hisako's father lounging in a deep armchair in his grand Western-style home and peeling skin off his infected feet.

"Mmm. . . People with athlete's foot should probably never take Turkish baths. The steam must make it unbearably itchy," said Gimpei and laughed mockingly. "Has anyone with athlete's foot been here before?"

"Well. . ."

The girl didn't seem to be trying to answer him seriously.

"People like us don't know what athlete's foot is, do we? It's only found on soft and pampered feet, isn't it? I mean, it's just a fact of life—coarse infections grow on fine feet. The germs wouldn't live on our monkey-feet, even if we planted them there. The skin is too hard and thick." As he spoke, he remembered that the girl's white fingers had clung soft and moist to the soles of his ugly feet while she was rubbing them.

"Even athlete's foot wouldn't come near mine."

Gimpei frowned. Why, just when he was feeling comfortable, had he started talking about skin infections to this beautiful bath girl? Did he really have to bring it up? It must have been because he had lied to Hisako that day.

Gimpei had stood in front of Hisako's house and

asked her to find out the name of a certain medicine because he was suffering from athlete's foot. But it was a lie, it had just slipped out. This lie had been followed by another when he thanked Hisako three or four days later for his recovery. He did not have athlete's foot at all. It had been the truth when he had told his class that he knew nothing about it, and he had thrown away the medicine that Hisako gave him. And when he told the woman in the amusement quarter that he had athlete's foot and was virtually crippled by it, the chain of involuntary lies was merely reinforced. A lie, once told, never vanishes, but chases after us. Just as Gimpei followed women, so his lies trailed behind him. Perhaps it is the same with crime. A crime, once committed, pursues a person until he repeats it. Bad habits are like that. The first time Gimpei followed a woman led to the second, and so on. . . The need to follow women is as persistent as athlete's foot; it doesn't clear up, it spreads. One summer's infection can be temporarily cured, only to erupt again the following summer.

"I'm not suffering from athlete's foot, you know. I know nothing about it." Gimpei spat out the words as if to rebuke himself. Why had he ever compared the ecstasy of following a woman to a disgusting thing like athlete's foot? Had the first lie forced him to make the association?

But now a sudden thought flashed across Gimpei's

mind: was it, perhaps, the sense of shame he felt about his ugly feet that had made him suddenly mention this fictitious infection in front of Hisako's house? And if so, was his habit of chasing after women related to this ugliness, since it was his feet that did the chasing? He was surprised at the thought. Was the ugliness of a part of his body crying out, longing for beauty? Was it part of the divine plan that ugly feet chased beautiful women?

The girl at the bath massaged Gimpei from the knees down along his legs, turning her back to him. This position brought his feet just below her eyes.

"That's enough," Gimpei said nervously. He curled his long toes, bending them at their bony joints.

The girl then asked him in a beautiful, resonant voice:

"Shall I cut your nails for you?"

"Nails?. . . Oh! Toenails. . . Are you really going to cut them?" To cover his embarrassment, Gimpei added, "I'm sure they're very long, though, aren't they?"

The girl placed her palm against the sole of his foot, and with a light touch of her hand, stretched out his toes, which were curled up like a monkey's. "A bit long. . ."

She was gentle and careful cutting his nails.

"It's good that you're always here," Gimpei began to say. He had already yielded his toes to the woman's care. "I can come here whenever I want to see you. When I want to have you massage me I can call your number, can't I?"

"Yes."

"You aren't a casual passer-by. You're not a stranger whose name and address I don't know. You're not like those people whom I lose in the world and never see again unless I chase after them as they go by. This may sound strange. . ."

Never before had he exposed his ugly feet as completely as he had to this girl who was now cutting his toenails, holding his foot in her hand, and the thought brought warm tears of happiness to his eyes.

"This may sound strange, but I'm telling you the truth. Have you ever had that experience . . . a feeling of profound regret after passing some stranger in the street? I've had it often. I think to myself, 'What a delightful looking person!' or 'What a beautiful woman!' or 'I've never seen anyone quite as attractive as that before.' It happens when I'm just strolling around the streets, or sitting next to a stranger in the theater or walking down the steps from a concert hall. But once they've gone, I know I'll probably never meet them again in my life. . . One can't stop and suddenly speak to a complete stranger, can one? Perhaps that's life, but when it happens I could die of sadness. I feel somehow drained and empty. I want to follow them to the ends of the earth, but I can't. The only way to chase a person that way is to kill him."

Gimpei gulped, realizing that he had been carried away. He added evasively:

"Of course, I'm exaggerating a bit. Fortunately I can make a telephone call whenever I want to hear your voice. But unlike your customers, you have a problem, don't you? You may like one particular customer and look forward to him coming again, but it's up to him whether he returns or not and he may never come back. Don't you think it's sad sometimes? Still, I suppose it's inevitable."

Gimpei watched her shoulder blades move slightly across her girlish back as she clipped his toenails. When she had finished, she paused momentarily, with her back still turned.

"How about your fingers?" she asked and turned around. Gimpei looked at his hands, holding them above his chest.

"They haven't got such long nails as my toes, have they? Not as dirty, either."

His words did not, however, imply refusal, and so the girl also cut his fingernails.

Gimpei had already sensed that the bath girl felt there was something sinister about him. The words he had just uttered so thoughtlessly seemed gruesome even to himself. Would the ultimate end of a chase be murder? All he had done was pick up Miyako Mizuki's handbag, and it was unlikely he would ever see her again. Perhaps it was not very different from his other brief encounters with passing strangers. He had been cut off from Hisako Tamaki, too, and it was difficult to meet her. He hadn't tracked his women down to the end. He might already have lost both Hisako and Miyako in a world beyond his reach.

With amazing vividness the faces of Hisako and Yayoi appeared before his eyes, and Gimpei compared their faces with that of the bath girl's.

"It must be strange if a customer doesn't return after all this care and attention."

"Oh no. Why? It's just a job."

"To think that you can say 'It's just a job' in a voice like that."

The girl looked aside. Gimpei closed his eyes as if ashamed. Through the narrow opening between his lids he had a blurred vision of her white bra.

"Take it off," Gimpei had once said to Hisako, holding the edge of her bra. Hisako shook her head. He had grabbed it and jerked it forward so that the elastic snapped. Dazed, Hisako had left her breasts exposed and stared at the bra, which he held for a moment in his right hand and then threw aside.

He opened his eyes and looked at the girl's right hand clipping his nails. How much younger than this girl had Hisako been then? Two years? Three? Had Hisako's skin become as fair as the bath attendant's?

Gimpei could smell the dark blue dye of Kurume cotton with its splashed pattern. The kimono he had worn as a boy had been made of this cloth, but the smell was evoked by the color of the blue serge skirt of Hisako's school uniform. As she slipped her legs into the skirt, Hisako had wept and he himself had been close to tears.

Gimpei felt all the strength drain from the fingers in his right hand, which the girl held as she cut his nails skillfully with a pair of scissors. He recalled that this same hand had once gone limp while he was walking with Yayoi hand in hand across the ice on the lake in his mother's village.

"What's the matter?" Yayoi had asked and returned to the shore. If Gimpei had held her hand tightly enough, perhaps he could have drowned her underneath the ice.

Yayoi and Hisako were not casual passers-by. He not only knew their names and addresses, but had a relationship with them and could meet them at any time. Yet he had still chased them and, worse, he had been forced to part from them.

"How about your ears? Shall I clean them?" the girl asked.

"Ears? What are you going to do with them?"

"I'll clean them. Would you like to sit up?"

Gimpei sat up on the couch. He felt the girl delicately rub the lobe of his ear, then quickly insert a finger and twist it gently inside. The stale air was let out, and Gimpei felt his ear lighten and fill with subtle fragrance. Delicate, tremulous sounds were heard and their gentle vibrations spread as the sounds continued. The girl was apparently tapping the finger inside his ear lightly with her other hand.

"What are you doing? It's like a dream," Gimpei said from his strange ecstasy. He turned around, but of course he couldn't see his own ear. Then, bending her arm in slightly toward his face, the girl put her finger back in his ear and slowly turned it.

"It's like an angel's whisper of love. I only wish I could clean out all the other human voices that have lodged there, so that I could listen only to your beautiful voice. Even lies would vanish. . ."

The girl drew her half-naked body close to Gimpei's nakedness, and the heavenly music swelled within him.

"I hope you have enjoyed the service."

The massage was over. While Gimpei was still sitting down, the attendant helped him put on his socks, buttoned his shirt, slipped his shoes on and tied the laces for him. The only thing he did himself was adjust his belt and knot his tie. While he had a cold soft drink outside the bathroom the girl stood by his side.

Gimpei was led by the girl to the front door and, as he stepped out into the night-filled garden, he had a vision of a huge spider's web. Together with other insects, there were two or three white-eyes trapped in the web, and lovely white circles stood out on their blue wings and around their eyes. The strands would have snapped if they had moved their wings, but their wings were folded and the birds were slender prisoners in the web. The spider was in the middle with its back to the white-eyes, perhaps afraid that their beaks would pierce its body if it came too close to them.

Gimpei raised his eyes to the dark woods. A night fire on a distant shore glowed in the lake of his mother's village, and he felt mysteriously drawn toward the flames reflected in the blackness of the water.

After Miyako Mizuki had lost her handbag and the two hundred thousand yen it contained, she did not go to the police. It was indeed a large enough sum to seriously affect her life, but such were her circumstances that she found it inconvenient to report the loss. So Gimpei perhaps need not have fled, even as far as Shinshu, though it seemed it was the money itself, and not the theft, that pursued him in his wanderings.

There was no doubt that he had taken the money, but since he had called after Miyako when she dropped her bag, he might not perhaps have committed a robbery. Neither did Miyako think that she had been robbed by Gimpei. She hadn't admitted to herself that it was he who had taken her bag. When she had hurled it in the middle of the street, Gimpei had been the only person there, so it was quite natural to suspect him. But since Miyako did not see him take the thing, someone else might have picked it up.

As soon as she got in, Miyako called her maid.

"Sachiko! Sachiko! My handbag . . . I've lost it. Go and look for it, please. It should be in front of the

43

drugstore over there. Hurry up! Run!"

"Yes."

"If you don't go at once someone else might take it."

Miyako went upstairs, breathing heavily. The other maid, Tatsu, followed.

"Did you say that you'd lost your handbag, miss?"

Tatsu was Sachiko's mother. She had served in the house before she made her daughter work with her. Two maids were unnecessary in the small house of a single woman, but Tatsu had taken advantage of a moral ambiguity in the household and risen above the status of a servant. Sometimes Tatsu called Miyako "ma'am" and sometimes "miss," but when the old gentleman, Arita, called at the house, Tatsu always addressed her as "ma'am."

One day, in spite of herself, Miyako had felt an urge to confide in Tatsu.

"You know, when we were at a hotel in Kyoto, the maid assigned to us liked calling me 'miss' when I was alone with her. But when Arita was with me, she used 'ma'am,' even though I'm much younger than Arita. Calling me 'miss' could have shown she was slighting me, but I felt she was just pitying me, thinking 'Oh, you poor thing,' and it made me feel sad." To which Tatsu had replied, "Then I'll address you that way too," and since then she had always done so.

"But, miss, it's odd that you dropped your handbag and left it behind while walking along the street, isn't

44

it? You were only carrying your bag, weren't you? You didn't have anything else to hold."

Tatsu stared up at Miyako, her little eyes wide open.

Her eyes were round, even when they weren't wide open, and their very roundness made them look small and startled. When Sachiko, who looked just like her mother, opened hers wide they were beautiful; but when Tatsu's eyes widened they seemed to bulge, with something disquieting and secretive about them that suggested hidden depths. They were a very clear, pale brown, which gave her expression a certain coldness.

Her fair-skinned face was also small and round. The neck was thick, her breasts large, and her heaviness increased down to her small feet. Her daughter's tiny feet were exquisite, but Tatsu's seemed to scuttle beneath the bulk they carried. Both mother and daughter were short.

The fleshy nape of her neck made it difficult for Tatsu to bend her head backward, and she had to turn her eyes up to look at Miyako. This made Miyako feel as if Tatsu were looking straight through her.

"I told you, I dropped it," Miyako said in the tone she used for scolding servants. "To prove it, I don't have my handbag with me. Look!"

"But, miss, you said that you lost it in front of the drugstore over there, didn't you? You know where you lost it, and it's in this neighborhood. How can it be lost, then? A thing like a handbag. . ."

"I dropped it, I tell you."

"I could understand your leaving it behind some-where like an umbrella, but to let it just drop out of your hand. . . I mean, monkeys don't fall out of trees, do they?"

Tatsu had made a curious comparison.

"You could have picked it up when you realized you dropped it. Why didn't you?"

"Of course I could. What nonsense you talk! If you notice the moment you've dropped something, then you can't say you've really lost it, can you?"

Miyako realized that she had been standing in her street clothes since she came upstairs. Her wardrobe of Western dresses and her chest-of-drawers for Japanese clothes were in the upstairs four-and-a-half-mat room. It was convenient for Miyako to change in the room next to the eight-mat one which she and old Arita used when he came to stay. But the fact that she had her clothes upstairs also revealed the extent of Tatsu's influence on the floor below.

"Go downstairs and bring me a damp towel, please. Wring it out in cold water. I'm perspiring slightly." Miyako thought that her request would make Tatsu stay downstairs while she wiped the sweat off her body.

"Yes. Shall I rub you down? I'll bring a basin of water with ice cubes in it from the refrigerator."

"No thank you." Miyako frowned.

Just as Tatsu was coming down the stairs, the front door opened.

"Mother, I searched all the way from the front of the drugstore to the road with the streetcars, but the mistress's handbag wasn't there," Sachiko said.

"I'm not surprised. Run upstairs and tell the mistress. Did you report it to the police?"

"Do you think we should?"

"How can you be so thoughtless? Go and report it right away."

"Sachiko! Sachiko!" Miyako called from upstairs. "You don't have to report it. There's nothing important in the bag."

Sachiko did not answer, but Tatsu came up, holding a wooden tray with a washbasin on it. Miyako had taken off her skirt and was in her underwear.

"Would you like me to wipe your back, ma'am?" Tatsu asked with exaggerated politeness.

"No thank you."

Miyako wiped herself with the towel that she had asked Tatsu to wring out for her. She started from her outstretched legs and cleaned between her toes. Tatsu picked up the crumpled stockings Miyako had left on the floor and folded them neatly.

"No, you don't have to bother. I'm going to wash them," Miyako said and threw the towel toward Tatsu.

Sachiko came up. As she bowed very low with her

hand near the doorsill of the adjoining four-and-a-half-mat room she said, "I've come back. The bag wasn't there." She looked lovely, but slightly comical.

Tatsu had schooled her daughter strictly in such formalities, though she herself fluctuated in her attitude toward Miyako, switching from extreme politeness to downright rudeness or clammy friendliness, depending on the situation. She had taught Sachiko to tie old Arita's shoelaces for him when he was leaving. Arita suffered from neuralgia and would sometimes prop himself up with his hands on Sachiko's shoulders while she crouched at his feet. Miyako had long since seen through Tatsu's plan for her daughter to steal Arita away from her, but she wasn't yet certain whether Tatsu had instructed the seventeen-year-old girl in the scheme. Tatsu made Sachiko use perfume. When Miyako once asked about this Tatsu replied, "She has a strong body odor."

"Why don't you tell Sachiko to go to the police station and report it?" Tatsu pressed.

"You're too insistent."

"But don't you think it's a shame to lose it? How much money was in it?"

"There was no money in it." Miyako closed her eyes and placed the cold towel over them. She remained still for a while. Her heart began beating quickly again.

Miyako had two passbooks. One was for a deposit

account in Tatsu's name, kept secret from old Arita at the maid's suggestion. The other was in her own name, and it was with this one that Miyako had withdrawn the two hundred thousand yen. She hadn't told Tatsu about this. If old Arita were to hear about the loss, he might start asking questions, so she had to be careful not to reveal anything too soon.

The two hundred thousand yen was Miyako's compensation for the loss of her youth—that brief flowering which she had wasted by giving her body to a half-dead, gray-haired old man. Miyako's own blood had flowed into the money, but if the money was lost it had gone in a flash and she had nothing left. She could not believe it. When one spends money, one remembers spending it even after it's gone. But when one loses the money one has saved, the very thought of saving is a bitter memory.

Still, Miyako could not deny the fact that she had felt a momentary thrill when she lost the money—a thrill of pleasure. Rather than run away because she was frightened by the man following her, she may well have swung abruptly to one side, dodging the sudden upsurge of pleasure.

Of course Miyako knew she hadn't dropped her handbag. Just as it had been unclear to Gimpei whether the bag had been used to hit him or had been thrown at him, so Miyako found it hard to remember if she had struck the man or hurled the thing at him. But she had certainly reacted strongly. Her hand had suddenly become numb, and the numbness had spread to her arm and chest until her whole body was quivering with painful ecstasy. It was as if some vague sensation, smoldering within her while she was being followed by the man, had suddenly caught fire—almost as though her youth, lost in old Arita's shadow, had suddenly been restored to life and had taken its revenge. If this were true, Miyako, at that precise moment, received compensation for all the shame she had endured through the long days and months it had taken to accumulate the two hundred thousand yen. And so the money was probably not lost in vain.

But at the time, the two hundred thousand yen had had nothing to do with the incident. Miyako had completely forgotten about the money when she hit the man with the handbag or threw it at him. She did not even notice when the handbag left her hand. Furthermore, she did not remember the bag when she suddenly turned and started to run, and in this sense Miyako had been telling the truth when she said that she had dropped it. Even before striking the man she had actually forgotten both the bag and the money it contained. The idea that she was being followed by a man had borne down on her like an oncoming wave, and when the wave broke, the handbag was lost.

Miyako still felt the numb sensation of pleasure in her body when she entered the front door of her house, and that was why she had hurriedly and furtively gone upstairs.

"I'd like to undress by myself. So go downstairs, please," Miyako said to Tatsu after she had wiped her neck and arms.

"Why don't you do it in the bathroom?" Tatsu said, looking at Miyako suspiciously.

"I don't want to move."

"I see. But are you sure that you lost the bag in front of the drugstore . . . after you turned this way from the road with the streetcar tracks? . . . Perhaps I'll just go to the police station and inquire after all."

"I don't remember where I lost it."

"Why not?"

"Because I was being followed by. . ."

In her anxiety to be left alone so that she could wipe away all trace of her excitement, Miyako had made an awkward slip of the tongue.

"Again?" Tatsu's round eyes glared.

"Yes, I tell you," Miyako said emphatically. But no sooner had she said it than the lingering pleasure quickly evaporated, leaving her empty and cold.

"Did you come straight home today? Or did you walk back dragging a man behind you? That's why you lost your handbag, isn't it?"

Tatsu turned to Sachiko, who was still sitting there.

"Sachiko, what are you still hanging about here for?"

Sachiko's eyes looked dazzled, and she blushed when she staggered up on one leg to go.

Sachiko knew, however, that Miyako had been followed by men before. Old Arita also knew. Right in the center of Ginza, Miyako had whispered to the old man, "Look! Someone's following me!"

"What?" The old man started to turn round.

"No. Don't look."

"Why not? How do you know you're being followed?"

"Oh, I can see. It's the tall man wearing a bluish hat who just passed us from the opposite direction."

"I didn't notice. Did you give him a sign as he went by?"

"Don't be silly! Am I supposed to ask him whether he's just an ordinary passer-by or someone due to play a part in my life?"

"Are you pleased?"

"I'd like to ask him, actually. Let's have a bet on how far he'll follow me. I'd like to bet with you. But it won't work if I'm with an old man carrying a stick, so you go into that tailor's shop over there and watch him. If he follows me all the way to the end of the street and back I'll have a white summer suit made. But not linen, dear."

"If you lose? . . ."

"Let me see. You can rest your head on my arm all night."

"It's not fair if you look behind or speak to him, you know."

"Of course."

It was a bet that old Arita expected to lose. He thought Miyako would let him sleep all night with his head on her arm even if he lost. But when he considered that he would not know if she were still there or not while he was fast asleep, he smiled grimly to himself and entered the tailor's shop. As he watched Miyako and the man pursuing her, he felt a strange youthfulness flickering inside him. It was not jealousy. Jealousy was forbidden.

At home Arita kept a beautiful woman on the pretext of employing a housekeeper. She was in her thirties, over ten years older than Miyako. When his head was pillowed in the arms of these two women, his neck supported by them and their breasts in his mouth, old Arita, who was almost seventy, imagined the two young women were his mother. For only with a mother could the old man find peace of mind. He had made both Miyako and the housekeeper aware of each other's roles. He would frighten Miyako by saying that if the two of them became jealous, it might arouse his anger and make him so wild that he would injure them. Or it would bring on a heart attack, which would kill him. He sounded self-preoccupied, but Arita really did suffer from a persecution neurosis. Miyako knew his heart was weak because she used to press his chest firmly with her soft hands and gently place her beautiful cheek against it when he wished. But the housekeeper, who was called Umeko, did not seem entirely free from jealousy. From long experience, Miyako guessed that whenever Arita was too nice to her the moment he arrived at her place, he must have been chased out of his own house by Umeko's jealousy. The fact that the youthful Umeko could be so jealous of such an old man seemed shameful to Miyako and brought her to the point of utter despair.

As old Arita often praised Umeko as a paragon of domesticity, Miyako imagined that she herself was required to be some kind of "good time girl." But it was apparent that the old man longed for both women as mother figures. His own mother had been divorced when he was two years old, and a stepmother had appeared. The old man had told this story repeatedly to Miyako.

"How happy I would have been if someone like you or Umeko had come to look after me, even as a stepmother." The old man used to indulge himself childishly in Miyako's company.

"You can't tell. I would shout at you if you were my stepchild. You must have been a horrible boy."

"I was a lovely child."

"To make up for the ill treatment you suffered as a stepchild you now have a good mother—even two—in your old age. You *are* lucky, aren't you?" Miyako said somewhat cynically.

"I certainly am. I'm grateful," Arita answered.

"How can he say 'I'm grateful,' indeed?" Miyako thought to herself, and anger stirred within her. But at the same time she couldn't help feeling that something was to be learned about life from such behavior in a hard-working old man of close on seventy.

Arita seemed to get impatient with the idle life Miyako led. Left to herself Miyako had no work to do. She was losing her youth and energy, spending her life in aimless anticipation of an old man's visits. Miyako wondered how her maid Tatsu could be so enthusiastic. It was she who had suggested that Miyako, whom the old man always took with him on his trips, should alter the hotel bills. Tatsu told her to have the bills made out for more than the real amount and then to arrange for the surplus to be returned to her. But Miyako felt that this finagling would depress her even if there were a hotel that would agree to carry out such an arrangement.

"If you feel that way, then you can at least profit from his tips. You could pay the hotel bill in an adjoining room, ma'am. Make Mr. Arita fork out a handsome gratuity. He'll certainly part with a lot just for appearances' sake. Before you go into the room, just peel off, say, a thousand yen if he's given you three thousand, and put the money in your sash or under

55

your blouse and it won't be found."

"What an idea! I'm surprised at you. So greedy and mean. . ."

But considering the maid's salary, it couldn't be thought of simply as greed.

"It isn't mean, you know. You've no other way of making a nest egg except by watching every cent. Women like us have to hoard our money, day by day and month by month," Tatsu said emphatically. "I'm on your side, ma'am. How can I stand by watching your young life go to that greedy, blood-sucking old man?"

When Arita visited them, Tatsu changed her voice as readily as a shopgirl to please him. Just now she had spoken to Miyako in a sinister voice, and Miyako had suddenly felt cold. But it was not really her voice or her words that made Miyako shiver: it was cold dismay at the swiftness with which time was carrying away her own physical youth, compared to the time needed to laboriously build up her savings.

Miyako's upbringing had been different from Tatsu's. Until the end of the war Miyako had been raised in lavish surroundings, in a "bed of roses" as they say, and she could hardly be expected to filch money from a hotel bill. Miyako decided that the scurrilous advice Tatsu had given her could be taken as evidence that her maid was pilfering things from the kitchen.

Even when she sent Tatsu for some medicine for colds, it cost five or ten yen more than when she asked Sachiko to get it. Miyako was curious to find out through Sachiko how much Tatsu had managed to save by accumulating these small amounts, but as there was no indication that Tatsu even gave her daughter an allowance, it was unlikely that she had shown her her passbook. Miyako made light of these small deceits, but she found it hard to overlook the implications of Tatsu's antlike thrift. Tatsu's life could be seen as a kind of healthiness and Miyako's as a disease. Miyako's youth and beauty were being frittered away, while Tatsu seemed to live without losing even a tiny part of herself. When Miyako heard Tatsu say that her husband, who was killed in the war, had given her a hard time, Miyako asked eagerly, "Did he make you cry?"

"Oh, yes! Did I cry! I'd say that not a day passed without my eyes getting red and swollen from crying. He threw some fire tongs once at Sachiko and they hit her on the neck. The small scar's still there, at the back of her neck. You can see it. I think this scar is the strongest evidence."

"Evidence of what?"

"Well, miss, how could I explain?"

"Men must be dreadful when even someone like you was bullied," Miyako declared with feigned naiveté.

"Yes, indeed! But there's another way of looking at it. At the time it was like being hypnotized by a fox. I was so wrapped up in my husband that I couldn't look anywhere else. But once we were free of the spell, everything was all right."

Miyako found that Tatsu's words conjured up memories of herself as a girl who had lost her first love to the war.

Brought up in luxury, Miyako was somewhat indifferent to money, and though two hundred thousand yen was a large sum for her now, she was resigned to the loss. After all, Miyako's family had lost incomparably more than two hundred thousand in the war. But the fact remained that there was now no way for her to make up even this kind of sum. She had no idea what to do, for she had taken the money out of her bank account for a particular need. Since it was such a large amount it might be advertised in the newspaper if it was found and reported. And as there was a passbook in the handbag, the name and address could be checked, and the person who picked it up could bring it directly to her home, or the police might notify her. Miyako scanned the newspapers carefully for three or four days. She realized that her name and address were also known to the man who had followed her. She wondered whether it was really he who had stolen the bag? If not, he would surely have followed her further, whether he had picked it up or not. Perhaps he had run off in shock after being struck by the bag?

It was about a week after Miyako made Arita buy her the white summer-suit material in Ginza that she lost her handbag. During that week the old man did not come to Miyako's place. He showed up at night two days after the handbag incident.

"How pleased we are to see you again." Tatsu welcomed him cheerfully and took his wet umbrella. "Did you walk, sir?"

"Yes. The weather's wretched. I suppose we're now in the rainy season."

"It's brought on your pains, hasn't it, sir?... Sachiko! Sachiko!" Tatsu called, and added, "She's taking a bath." She stepped down in bare feet to the porch to help the old man take off his shoes.

"If the bath's ready, I'd like to warm myself up. When it gets damp and unseasonably chilly like today..."

"I imagine it affects you, sir." Her short eyebrows knitted in sympathy above her beady eyes. "Oh dear, what a nuisance. Since we didn't expect you tonight, Sachiko's got in the bath before you. What am I to do?"

"It's all right."

"Sachiko! Sachiko! Get out of the bath right away. Scoop the surface off carefully, will you? Leave it clean ... wash well all around..." Tatsu bustled off

59

and only came back after she had put the kettle on the stove and turned on the gas for the bath.

Old Arita, still in his raincoat, was rubbing his legs, which were stretched out on the floor.

"Do you want Sachiko to rub you while you're in the bath?"

"Where's Miyako?"

"Well, madam said that she was going to a news theater. I think she'll be back soon, as she went to the cinema just for the news."

"Send for a masseuse, will you?"

"Yes, sir. Your usual masseuse?..." Tatsu stood up and went to fetch the old man's clothes.

"You usually change in the bathroom, don't you?" she asked on her return. Tatsu called out "Sachiko!" once more, then said, "Now I'm going to fetch the masseuse."

"Has Sachiko got out yet?"

"Yes, she has, sir... Sachiko!"

When Miyako came home about an hour later, old Arita was being massaged by a woman in the bedroom upstairs.

"I have pains," he said in a low voice. "Why did you go out in this nasty rain? Take a bath and you'll feel refreshed."

"All right."

Miyako sat down and for no particular reason leaned against the wardrobe. She had not seen Arita for about a week, and his complexion seemed to have become ashen and dull. Pale brown spots were prominent on his cheeks and hands.

"I went to see a newsreel. I feel excited watching the news. On my way there I thought of giving up the news to have my hair washed, but the beauty parlor was already closed, so. . ." Miyako glanced at the old man's hair, which looked as if it had just been washed.

"I can smell your hair tonic."

"Sachiko wears a lot of perfume, doesn't she?"

"I heard she has a strong body odor."

"Hmm."

Miyako went downstairs to the bathroom and washed her hair. Calling for Sachiko, she had her rub it with a dry towel.

"What lovely feet you have!" said Miyako, her elbows on her knees, stretching out a hand to touch Sachiko's instep which was just in front of her eyes. She felt the girl's shudder across her own bare shoulders. Sachiko, perhaps inheriting her mother's nature, also seemed to have light fingers, but the only things she stole from Miyako were used lipsticks, broken combs that Miyako discarded in her wastepaper basket, or dropped hairpins. Miyako was aware that this was because the girl adored and envied her beauty.

After the bath, Miyako, wearing a light coat over a cotton kimono with a thistle pattern on a white background, rubbed the old man's legs. She wondered if this would become her daily chore if she moved into his house.

"Is that masseuse good?"

"No, she's not. The one who comes to my place is better—more experienced and conscientious."

"A woman?"

"Yes."

The realization that massage must also be daily work for Umeko, the housekeeper, made Miyako feel disgusted and her hands lost their strength. Arita took her finger and pressed it into the dent at the base of his spine. Miyako's finger bent backward.

"Long, slender fingers like mine are not much good, I suppose."

"Well . . . not really, perhaps. But a young, affectionate girl's fingers are good all the same."

Miyako felt a shiver run down her spine, and her finger slipped out of the dent. The old man caught hold of her finger again.

"Don't you think short fingers like Sachiko's are better? Why don't you let Sachiko have some practice?"

The old man remained silent. Miyako suddenly recalled a passage from Radiguet's *Le Diable au corps*. She had read the novel after seeing the film. " 'I don't want to make your life unhappy. I'm crying because I'm too old for you!' Marthe said. This expression of

62

love was sublime in its childishness. And whatever passions I was to experience after this, it would never be possible to recapture the exquisite emotion of seeing a nineteen-year-old girl crying because she thought she was too old." Marthe's lover was sixteen years old. At nineteen Marthe herself was much younger than Miyako, who was twenty-five; and, aware that her own youth was quickly fading at the hands of this old man, Miyako had been profoundly disturbed when she read the passage. Arita always said that Miyako looked younger than her age, and it was not just in the old man's favorably prejudiced eyes that this seemed true, for everyone thought Miyako younger than she really was. But Miyako could see that the old man's covetous delight in her youth made him speak of how young she was. He was afraid that her fresh, young features would disappear and that the muscles of her body would one day lose their firmness. It might be considered strange and indecent that a man who was close on seventy should demand still more youth in his twenty-five-year-old mistress, but Miyako would often forget to be critical of the old man and, stimulated by his enthusiasm, wished she could be more youthful herself. While coveting her youth, Arita, at the same time, thirsted for Miyako's maternal affection. Without intending to respond, Miyako sometimes had the illusion that she really was a mother.

While he was lying stretched out on his face, she pressed her thumbs against his hips. Miyako leaned slightly forward with her breasts thrust out.

"Couldn't you try getting on my hips?" Arita said. "You could step on them gently, couldn't you?"

"No, I don't want to. . . Let Sachiko do it for you. She'd be good because she's tiny and has small feet."

"She's a child. She'll feel shy."

"I feel shy, too," she said, thinking that Sachiko was two years younger than Marthe and one year older than Marthe's lover. But what of it?

"You stayed away because you lost the bet, didn't you?"

"Oh, that," the old man said, turning his head like a snapping turtle. "No, it was my neuralgia."

"Then it must be because you prefer the masseuse who comes to your house."

"Hmm . . . perhaps. Besides, you wouldn't let me sleep with my head on your arm because I lost the bet."

"Oh, all right. I'll let you."

Miyako was well aware that Arita had come to find the pleasure of having his legs and thighs rubbed or burying his face in her breasts a more suitable pastime for his age. The busy old man referred to these gratifying hours at Miyako's house as "the slave's emancipation." The words reminded Miyako of her own hours of slavery.

"If you're in a cotton kimono you'll catch cold after your bath. Thank you, that's enough," Arita said, rolling over on his side. As she had expected, her offer of an arm for a pillow was effective. She was tired of massaging.

"Anyway, how do you feel having a man like the one in the blue hat follow you?"

"Oh, very pleasant. The color of his hat has nothing to do with it," she replied in a deliberately lively voice.

"Yes, I suppose it doesn't if all the man did was follow you, but. . ."

"The day before yesterday I was followed by a strange man as far as the neighborhood drugstore and I lost my handbag. I was frightened."

"What? Two men in one week?"

Miyako nodded as she allowed Arita to rest his head on her arm. Unlike Tatsu the old man did not seem to find it strange that she had dropped her handbag while out walking. He might have been so surprised at her being followed by another man that he forgot to be suspicious. His surprise generated a feeling of pleasure in Miyako, and her body relaxed. Arita buried his face in her breasts and pressed the warm shapes against his forehead with his hands.

"Mine."

"Yes, yours," Miyako answered promptly, like a child, and tears started swimming in her eyes as she lay motionless looking down at the old, gray head. She turned off the light. Floating in the darkness, the face of the man who had picked up her handbag appeared, a face which had seemed to weep the moment he decided to follow her.

"Ah. . ." he must have groaned. Though scarcely audible, Miyako was sure she had heard it.

And in her mind's eye she saw him stop to look back after passing her; and in a flash the luster of her hair, the color of her flesh at the ears and neck had struck him with a piercing sorrow and, fainting, drawn that stifled cry from his heart. Hearing him groan, Miyako glanced back at his broken face, and at that precise moment the decision was made that he would follow her. He looked sad, lost in his own world. Miyako felt as if the darkness in him had escaped and passed on into her.

Miyako had only glanced back once at the beginning and did not look around again. Nor could she remember his appearance. She still saw, floating in the darkness, only the blurred distortion of his face as he struggled with his tears.

"You are wicked, aren't you?" Arita muttered a little later. Miyako made no reply, for she was choked with tears.

"You're an evil woman. Imagine being followed by so many men. . . Aren't you frightened of yourself? There must be some devil hidden in you."

"Ouch!" Miyako stiffened.

66

She remembered when, early one spring, her breasts had begun to hurt. She felt as if she could see her own body in its former immaculate nakedness. Though she looked younger than her age, physically she had completely matured into womanhood.

"How spiteful you are! It must be your neuralgia." Her mind was elsewhere. She was thinking how a gentle girl had grown into a spiteful woman as her body changed.

"Why spiteful?" old Arita replied squarely. "Do you find it fun to have a man follow you?"

"No, it isn't fun."

"But you said that you felt pleasure, didn't you? Probably because your association with an old man like me makes you feel bitter and vindictive."

"Vindictive about what?"

"About your life or misfortunes, I imagine."

"Whether I enjoy it or not . . . it isn't that simple."

"No, it's certainly not simple. It isn't easy to take revenge on one's life."

"Are you taking revenge on your life by going about with a young woman like me?"

"Hmm?" The old man was stuck for words, but went on. "No, it's not revenge that I'm taking. If you insist on calling it that, then I suppose I'm the one who's being attacked and on whom revenge is being taken."

Miyako was not paying attention. She was thinking

67

that, since she had already told him about losing her handbag, she might as well mention that a large sum of money had been inside it, so that he could compensate her for the loss. But two hundred thousand yen was too large an amount. How much should she ask for? Though the old man had supplied the money, she could do with it as she wished, for it was her savings. She'd be able to ask him for help quite easily by telling him that the money was to be used to help her brother get into university.

Even when they were children, people often said that she and her brother should have changed sex. But since she had become Arita's mistress, Miyako had grown indolent and timid, probably because she had lost all hope. When she read old proverbs like, "One can fuss about the beauty of a mistress, but it never mattered in a wife," she felt overwhelmed with sorrow, as though a curtain of darkness had dropped over her. She had lost her pride in her looks. Whenever she was followed by a man, this pride would surge up again, but Miyako knew that her beauty was not the only reason why men chased her. As Arita had said, there might be some evil spirit in her struggling to get out.

"Anyway, you're playing with fire," the old man said. "To be followed by men so often—it's courting the devil, you know."

"Yes, it must be," Miyako answered meekly.

"Perhaps there's a race of devils living among men but quite different from them, and perhaps they have a quite separate world of their own."

"Are you talking from personal experience? You frighten me. You could come to some harm. I tell you, you won't die an ordinary death."

"I wonder if something of the sort might not happen to the children in our family. Even my younger brother, who's as gentle as a girl, has written a will."

"Why?..."

"It was just a trifling matter—simply that he thought he couldn't afford to go to the same university as his best friend. It happened this spring. His friend Mizuno comes from a well-to-do family and, besides, he's bright. He said he would help my brother in the entrance examination and even write down the answers for him. My brother does well at school, too, but he's so timid that he thought he might get one of his fainting fits during the examination, which he did. The prospect of not entering even if he passed the exam might have made him more nervous, I think."

"You never told me that story before."

"I didn't think there was any point in telling you."

After a pause she continued.

"His friend Mizuno had no trouble because he's clever and works hard, but my mother had to pay to have my brother admitted. To celebrate his matriculation I invited them to dinner at Ueno, and then we all went to see the cherry blossoms at night in the zoo. I mean, with my brother, Mizuno and his girlfriend."

"Really?"

"I say 'girlfriend,' but she's still only fifteen. At the zoo where we saw the cherry blossoms, I was followed by a man. He was with his wife and child, but to my surprise he left them and chased me."

"Why do you do this sort of thing?" Arita was apparently astonished.

"Do I?... I felt jealous of Mizuno and his girl, and I suppose I looked sad, that's all. It's not my fault."

"Yes, it is your fault. You enjoy it, don't you?"

"That's too harsh. I never enjoy it, I assure you. On the day I lost my handbag, I was so scared I hit the man with it. Or I might have thrown it at him. I'm not sure which because I was so upset. There was a great deal of money in the bag—at least, for me it was a lot. I had been to the bank and taken out some cash to give to my mother. She needed it to repay a friend of my father's who had lent her money to get my brother into university."

"How much did you have in it."

"A hundred thousand yen." Miyako named half the amount impulsively, then held her breath.

"Hmm. That's a lot of money. So you had it stolen by a man, eh?"

Miyako nodded in the dark. Arita could feel her shoulders jerk and her heart throbbing. But Miyako was ashamed of having revealed half the sum, and her shame was tinged with fear. The old man's hands caressed her tenderly. Miyako knew that he was going to give her at least half the sum, yet she wept again.

"You don't have to cry. But if you go on doing that sort of thing you'll run into serious trouble one day. There are a lot of contradictions in what you tell me about being followed by men. Can't you see?" Arita reproached her gently.

He fell asleep with his head on Miyako's arm, but Miyako could not sleep. The early summer rain continued to fall. As she lay there, the thought crossed her mind that one couldn't tell Arita's age simply by listening to his breathing while he was asleep. Miyako pulled her arm away. As she did so she raised his head gently with her other hand, but he did not wake. She thought of the word he had just used and the contradiction implied in this old misogynist's sleeping next to her, entrusting himself completely to a woman. Her thoughts led Miyako back to her own self-loathing. Without being told, she knew how much he hated women. His wife had killed herself in a fit of jealousy when he was still in his thirties. Since then the horror of a woman's jealousy seemed to have imprinted itself so deeply on his mind that when a woman displayed the least sign of it, Arita held himself a thousand miles away. Either due to pride or despair, Miyako would never allow herself to feel jealous over Arita. But being a woman, a jealous phrase would sometimes slip out, and then old Arita would make such a disagreeable face that her jealousy would freeze and turn to desolation. But the old man's dislike of women did not seem to be entirely due to his fear of jealousy. Nor did it seem to stem from age. Miyako wondered how a woman could feel jealous of a man who was by nature averse to women, and she chided herself for her own feelings. But when she thought of the difference between their ages, she found it ridiculous to suppose that he could either hate or love women.

Miyako recalled her brother's friend and his sweetheart with some envy. She had heard from Keisuke that Mizuno had a girlfriend called Machie, but she only saw the girl for the first time on the day they celebrated their matriculation.

"I've never seen such an innocent beauty," Keisuke had once said.

"Isn't she precocious to have a lover at fifteen?" Miyako replied, and added as if to correct herself, "But she's seventeen when you count by the calendar year, isn't she? To think that girls of fifteen can have lovers nowadays! How lucky they are! But Kei, do you think you really understand what innocent beauty is in

72

a woman? I don't think you can see it just by looking."

"Oh yes, I can."

"But what does it consist of? Tell me."

"How can I answer a question like that?"

"She seems pure and lovely just because you think she is, doesn't she?"

"I'm sure you'll understand when you see her."

"Women are cruel, you know. They're not as soft as you are, Kei."

Perhaps because he remembered what his sister had said, it was Keisuke and not his friend who was awkward and blushing at their mother's home when Miyako first met Machie. As she could not ask her brother's friends to her place, Miyako had arranged for them all to meet at her mother's.

"I'll like her too, Kei," Miyako had told her brother in a back room as she helped him put on his new university uniform.

"Ah, I see! I should have put my socks on first." Keisuke sat down on the floor. Miyako sat down in front of him with her blue pleated skirt spread out.

"Don't forget to congratulate Mizuno, will you? I told him to bring Machie along."

"Yes, of course."

Miyako felt sorry for her shy brother because she suspected he was also fond of Machie.

"Mizuno's family strongly disapproves of their love and wrote to Machie's parents, you know. I heard they were furious at getting such an offensive letter. Machie's coming along secretly today," Keisuke said excitedly.

Machie was in the sailor blouse she wore as a student. She brought a small bunch of sweet peas for Keisuke to congratulate him on his entrance to university. The bouquet was placed in a glass vase on Keisuke's desk.

Miyako invited them to a Chinese restaurant in Ueno so that they could look at the cherry blossoms at night in Ueno Park. The park was thronged with people, the cherry trees looked tired, and the flowering branches were not fully grown. Even so, the color of the flowers deepened to pink in the electric light. Whether she was naturally quiet or simply deferring to Miyako, Machie did not talk much. She said that when she woke up in the morning the cherry blossoms in her garden were a beautiful sight, with petals strewn all over the pruned azalea bushes below. She also mentioned that she had seen the setting sun on her way to Keisuke's house, floating like the yellow yolk of a soft-boiled egg among the blossoms of the cherry trees that lined the moat.

While they were walking down the dark, lonely stone steps beside Kiyomizu Hall, Miyako spoke to Machie: "I think it was probably when I was three or four years old. . . I remember coming to this hall with my mother to hang up some paper cranes I had made so that my father would recover from his illness."

Machie was silent, but stopped with Miyako on their way down the steps and looked at Kiyomizu Hall.

The road in front of them, which led to the museum, was so crowded that they turned in the direction of the zoo. Seeing torches blazing along the stone-flagged approach to Tosho Shrine, they set off up it. Beside the road, stone lanterns stood silhouetted against the torchlight, and long sprays of cherry blossoms reached out above them. People who had come to look at the flowers sat in circles in an empty lot behind the lanterns. They were drinking, and there were candles burning in the middle of the groups.

Whenever a drunkard staggered toward them, Mizuno shielded Machie by hiding her behind him. Keisuke, a little apart from the other two, stood between them and the drunk as if to protect them both. As she held onto his shoulder to avoid the man, Miyako was surprised that Keisuke could be so brave.

In the light of the torches Machie's features stood out in greater beauty. Her face was grave, her lips tightly pressed together, and the color of her cheeks made one think of a girl praying in candlelight.

"Miyako," Machie said, suddenly hiding behind Miyako and clinging to her.

"What's the matter?"

"My schoolfriend . . . over there, with her father. They live close to my house."

75

"But why should you hide?" Miyako said. As she looked around, she took Machie's hand and held onto it while they walked along. Though they were both women, Miyako almost gave a little cry of joy when she touched Machie's hand, so pleasant was the sensation. She felt it lying soft and moist in hers, and was deeply moved by the young girl's beauty. But all she could say was, "Machie, you look happy."

Machie shook her head.

"Oh, why not?" Miyako looked into Machie's face with surprise. Her eyes were shining in the torchlight. "Can even you have known unhappiness?"

Machie was silent and let her hand drop. Miyako wondered how many years had passed since she had last walked hand in hand with another girl.

As she had often met Mizuno before, her attention that night was focused entirely on Machie, and while she was looking at the girl, a great sadness welled up in her that made her wish she were alone and far away. If she ever passed Machie in the street, she knew she would turn and stare at her retreating figure. Did men follow Miyako because they were drawn by a similar yet far more powerful feeling?

At the sound of a pot falling or being knocked over in the kitchen, Miyako's thoughts returned to the present. The mice must be out again. She hesitated, uncertain whether to get up and go into the kitchen. There might be more than one mouse there—perhaps even three. As she thought of their small, sleek bodies, soaked in the season's rain, Miyako put her hand up to her own damp hair and pressed it softly, feeling the coldness.

Old Arita moved as though he had a weight on his chest. His contortions became violent. Another dream, Miyako thought, and moved to one side frowning. The old man often had nightmares, and she was used to these disturbances. His shoulders rose and fell as though he were being strangled, and he swept at something with his arm and struck Miyako roughly across the neck. The groaning continued. She should have shaken him, but her body remained stiff and motionless, and a faintly cruel impulse rose up in her.

"Aaah, aaah!" the old man shouted as his arms swam about seeking Miyako's body in his dream. Sometimes, if he clung to Miyako, he would calm down without waking, but tonight his own screaming forced him awake.

"Ah!" After shaking his head he drew close to Miyako, exhausted. Her body softened tenderly. Used to this recurring nightmare, Miyako did not even bother to say, as she had once done, "Did you have a horrible dream? You've been tormented."

The old man, however, asked uneasily, "Did I say anything?"

"No, you didn't. You were just having a bad dream, dear."

"I see. Have you been awake all the time?"

"Yes, dear, I have."

"Really? Thank you."

The old man pulled Miyako's arm under his neck.

"This gets worse in the rainy season. It might also be the reason why you can't sleep." He added as if ashamed, "I thought my shouting woke you up."

"I always wake up for you, even in a deep sleep."

Old Arita's screams had been so loud that even Sachiko, sleeping downstairs, awoke.

"Mother! Mother! I'm scared." Sachiko clung to Tatsu in alarm. Tatsu caught her by the shoulder and pushed her away.

"There's no need to be frightened. It's only the master. It's he who's frightened, you see. That's why he can never sleep alone. You know how he takes our mistress with him on trips and treats her with such care. If he didn't suffer like this, he'd be too old to want a woman. He's simply having bad dreams, and there's nothing to be frightened about."

Six or seven children were romping about on a slope.
A few of them were girls, and the children seemed to
be on their way home from kindergarten. Some held
sticks and those that didn't were pretending to; and
they all tottered along with bent backs as though
leaning heavily on the sticks, singing in chorus as they
went: "Grandpa, Grandma lost their legs. . . Grandpa,
Grandma lost their legs. . ." These were the only
words they sang. For some reason the children looked
oddly earnest, engrossed in their antics, and gradually
their gestures became more exaggerated and violent.
One girl reeled along so wildly that she fell down.

"Wow! Ouch! Ouch!" The girl rubbed her back
as an old woman would. But when she got up she
rejoined the chorus: "Grandpa, Grandma lost their
legs. . ."

On top of the slope rose a high bank where a few
isolated pines stood among the new grass. The trees
were not tall, and their branches, shaped like those
seen in old screens or sliding doors, floated in the
spring evening sky.

The children walked up toward the sky, tottering

79

along the center of the slope. Wild as their antics were, they were in no danger from passing cars, for there was little traffic and few people about. It is still possible to find such places even in the residential districts around Tokyo.

There was only a girl with a dog coming up from the bottom of the slope. No—there was one other person, Gimpei Momoi, following her, but it's doubtful whether he could be counted as a whole person, for Gimpei was utterly lost in the girl.

She was walking in the leafy shade of the ginkgo trees that lined the sidewalk on one side of the road. The stone wall of a large residence rose abruptly on the other side and stretched along the entire slope. Opposite it, set far back from the road, stood the mansion of a prewar aristocrat with a stone wall built along a deep ditch like a miniature castle moat. Behind the wall of the estate, a mound rose gently to a grove of small pines, whose branches still bore the marks of careful pruning. A low, white, tile-roofed wall was visible above the pine grove. The ginkgo trees along the road were tall, and their first tiny leaves were still not dense enough to hide the branches. The setting sun shone through the leaves in pale and darker shades, depending on the height of each leaf and the way it faced. The girl was bathed in fresh green light.

She was dressed in a white woolen sweater and a

pair of rough cotton jeans, which were faded and gray, but had bright red checks on the cuffs. She wore her jeans a little short, and her fair skin peeped out above her canvas shoes. Her hair was tied back loosely in a ponytail, revealing the long, delicate curve of her neck. Her shoulders were pulled forward by the dog tugging at the rope. Gimpei was lost in her dreamlike beauty, and even the color of the skin which showed between the red checks and her white shoes weighed so heavily on his heart that he felt like dying or killing her. He remembered Yayoi in his home village and Hisako Tamaki, his student, but they were no match for this girl. Yayoi was fair, but her skin had no luster. Hisako's was dark and shiny, but the color was not clear, nor did it have the heavenly fragrance of this girl's skin. Gimpei felt shattered, heartbroken. Never again could he be the boy who had played with Yayoi or the teacher who had been in love with Hisako. Though it was a spring evening, Gimpei felt tears pricking his tired eyelids as if he were walking against a cold wind, and his breath was short even on the gentle upward slope. Weak and numb below the knees, he could not catch up with the girl. He had not seen her face yet. He wanted only to walk beside her to the top of the slope and talk to her about . . . well, about the dog, perhaps. There would be no other opportunity, and it seemed unbelievable to Gimpei that even this chance existed.

He raised his open hand and waved it about. It was partly a habit he had when remonstrating with himself as he walked along, but it was also because something had brought back the feeling he had had as a child when he had picked up the warm corpse of a mouse. Its eyes were fixed in a stare and its mouth dripped blood. A terrier at Yayoi's home near the lake had caught the mouse in the kitchen. Holding it in its jaws, the dog had stood there, not knowing quite what to do with it, until it dropped it meekly when Yayoi's mother said something to the dog and slapped it on the head. When the mouse fell on the wooden floor and the dog was about to spring on it, Yayoi picked up the terrier in her arms.

"That's enough, now! Well done! Good dog!" Yayoi cuddled it, then ordered Gimpei to take the mouse away.

He picked it up hastily and saw that one or two drops of blood had fallen from its mouth onto the wooden floor. The warmth of its body sent tingles down his spine, but though its eyes were vacant and staring, there was still something beautiful about them.

"Quickly now, go and throw it away!"

"Where?"

"Why not in the lake?"

Dangling the mouse by its tail, Gimpei took it to the shore of the lake and threw it out as far and as hard as he could. In the dark night he heard a forlorn, watery plop, then ran home at top speed. He felt bitter at Yayoi for having made him do it—after all, she was only a cousin, the child of his mother's elder brother. He had been twelve or thirteen at the time, and had had an awful dream about being chased by a mouse.

After it caught its first mouse, the terrier kept a sharp lookout in the kitchen every day as if this was the only thing it had ever learned. Whatever anyone said to the dog, it must have sounded like "mouse," for it would dash off into the kitchen at once. Whenever it was missing, it could be found lurking there in a corner. But it was no cat. Staring up at a mouse scurrying from the shelf up a pillar, the terrier would shriek hysterically. The color of its eyes would change, its expression became sick and neurotic, and Gimpei began to loathe the animal and its obsession. He stole a needle and some red thread from Yayoi's needlework box and waited for a chance to stick the needle through the terrier's thin ear. He decided it would be best to do it just before leaving, for there would be a fuss when they found the needle and red thread dangling from the dog's ear and they would think it was Yayoi's doing. But when Gimpei tried to stab the needle through its ear, the dog ran off screaming. Knowing he had failed, he hid the needle in his pocket and went home, then drew a picture of Yayoi and her dog, added several stitches of red thread and put it in the drawer of his desk.

It was his need to talk to the girl, using her dog or a similar subject as an excuse for conversation, that had made Gimpei remember the terrier which had caught the mouse, but he didn't really like dogs and had nothing interesting to say about them. Anyway, he was sure the girl's dog would bite him if he came too close, though this was not the reason why he was unable to catch up with the girl.

While she was walking along, she stooped to unfasten the rope from the dog's collar. Once released, the animal ran ahead of the girl, then flew back past her and up to Gimpei's feet. It started sniffing at his shoes.

"Hey!" Gimpei jumped back with a cry.

"Fuku! Fuku!" the girl called to the dog.

"Good God! Help!"

"Fuku!" she called again, and the dog ran back.

The color had drained from Gimpei's face.

"Phew! That was scaring!" Gimpei staggered and sat down. He deliberately exaggerated his movements to attract the girl's attention, but since he also felt genuinely dizzy, he closed his eyes. His heart was throbbing violently and he felt sick. Holding his forehead in his hands, he opened his eyes a little and saw the girl going up the slope without looking back, with the dog on the leash again.

An angry wave of humiliation swept over him. He thought the dog must have sniffed at his shoes because it knew how ugly his feet were.

"Damn it! I'll sew up that dog's ear too," he muttered and ran off up the slope. But his anger had abated by the time he caught up with the girl.

"Excuse me, miss!" he called out in a hoarse voice.

When the girl turned around, moving only her head, the ponytail swung out to reveal the beautiful nape of her neck. Gimpei's pale face blazed.

"What a lovely dog, miss. What kind is it?"

"A Japanese *shiba*."

"Where's it from?"

"From Koshu."

"It's your own dog, isn't it? Do you take it for a walk at the same time every day?"

"Yes."

"Always along this road?"

The girl did not answer, but she didn't seem particularly suspicious of Gimpei. He looked back down the slope and wondered which house was hers. He felt there must be peaceful and happy homes there among the young leaves.

"Does your dog catch mice?"

The girl did not so much as smile.

"It's cats that catch mice, isn't it? But a dog can, too, you know. The one we had in our house years ago was good at catching mice."

The girl did not even glance at Gimpei.

"But dogs don't eat the mice they catch, do they?...
I was still a child then, and I hated having to throw the
mouse away."

Gimpei was astonished at himself for telling such a
revolting story, yet the dead mouse floated before his
eyes, blood trickling from its mouth and its white,
clenched teeth just visible.

"The dog was a kind of terrier. It had thin bowlegs
that trembled. I didn't like it. There are as many kinds
of dogs as human beings, aren't there? How lucky this
dog is to walk with you!" Perhaps because he had
forgotten his recent fright, Gimpei bent over the dog
and was about to stroke its back when the girl quickly
shifted the leash from her right hand to her left and
moved the dog out of Gimpei's reach. As he saw the
shape of the dog move in front of him, Gimpei barely
suppressed the urge to put his arm round the girl's
legs. But before he could do anything rash, the sudden
realization that, every evening, she would walk here
with her dog beneath the shade of the ginkgo trees and
that he could watch her from a hiding place on
top of the bank came to him like a ray of hope. It was
like lying naked in the new grass, so cool and fresh was
his sense of relief. Yes, he would watch her from the
top of the bank, and she would come up the slope
toward him forever... His happiness knew no
bounds.

"You must forgive me. But your dog looked cute and I like dogs. . . It's only the ones that catch mice that I can't stand."

There was no reaction. When she reached the foot of the bank, the girl climbed on up the new grass with her dog. From the other side of the knoll a student appeared. Gimpei went weak with shock when he saw the girl stretch out her hand to the boy in greeting. Was she meeting him on the pretext of taking her dog for a walk? It dawned on Gimpei that the girl's dark eyes were liquid and shining with love. The sudden discovery numbed his brain, and her eyes became a black lake. He wanted to swim in her pure eyes, to bathe naked in the black lake, but he also felt a deep despair. He walked on sadly up the bank and lay down in the new grass, staring up at the sky.

The student was Mizuno, the friend of Miyako's younger brother, and the girl was Machie. It was about ten days before Miyako invited Machie and Mizuno to celebrate the boys' matriculation and see the Ueno cherry trees at night.

The moist light of Machie's black eyes looked beautiful to Mizuno, too. The dark pupils seemed to fill them entirely.

"I'd love to see you when you open your eyes first thing in the morning," Mizuno said, looking into them admiringly. He felt as if he were sinking into them. "Tell me how beautiful they are when you wake up."

87

"Sleepy, I should imagine."

"I'm sure they aren't. The minute I wake up I want to see you, Machie."

Machie nodded.

"At school, at least I could see you two hours after waking up."

"You said that once before, and since then, 'in two hours' time' has been my first thought, too, when I wake up."

"So your eyes don't look sleepy then?"

"I don't know."

"Isn't Japan wonderful? I mean, to have people with lovely black eyes like yours."

Her dark eyes enhanced the beauty of her lips and eyebrows. Her hair also seemed to glisten, matching the color of her eyes.

"When you left home did you tell them you were taking the dog for a walk?" Mizuno asked.

"No, I didn't. But I'm with the dog and it's obvious from the way I'm dressed."

"Isn't it risky to meet so near your house?"

"I feel bad about deceiving my family. If I don't take the dog, I can't get out. Even if I did manage to slip out they could easily guess where I'd been because I'd look embarrassed when I returned. But it's probably your family more than mine that will refuse permission."

"Don't let's talk about it. Both of us have to go back

to our homes, but it's silly to remember them while we're here. I suppose you can't stay long if you're just out with the dog, can you?"

Machie nodded. The two sat down on the fresh grass and Mizuno held the dog in his lap.

"Fuku knows you too, now."

"If dogs could speak, he might give the game away at home and then we wouldn't be able to see each other at all."

"Even if we couldn't, I'd wait. Anyway, I'm sure it'll be all right. I'm determined to get into your university. Then we can see each other 'in two hours' time' again, can't we?"

" 'In two hours' time' . . . well. . ." Mizuno mumbled. "I'm sure we can arrange it so that we don't even have to wait two hours."

"My mother thinks it's too soon and doesn't trust us. But I'm glad I met you too soon. I wish I could have known you when I was very young. If I'd met you in junior or primary school, I'm sure I'd have become just as fond of you, however small I was. They used to carry me piggyback up this slope when I was a baby and let me play on the bank. Did you ever come here when you were small?"

"I'm afraid I didn't."

"Really? I often think I might have met you on this slope when I was a baby. Perhaps that's why I've come to like you as much as I do now. . ."

"I wish I had come here when I was little."

"When I was a baby, strangers thought I was so sweet they used to pick me up and hold me in their arms. I had much bigger, rounder eyes in those days." Machie turned and looked at Mizuno with her large, black eyes.

"Some time ago, just when the middle schools were holding their graduation ceremonies, I was taking my dog for a walk. You know if you turn right at the bottom of this slope you come to the moat where they hire out boats? Well, as I was passing, I saw some boys and girls there who looked like this year's graduates, and they were sitting in a boat with their diplomas rolled up in their hands. I envied them celebrating the day in this way. There were girls leaning on the railings holding their diplomas and looking at their friends in the boat. I hadn't met you when I left junior school. I suppose you must have had another girlfriend then."

"No. I wasn't going out with any girls."

"Really?..." Machie tilted her head sideways. "You know, there are lots of wild ducks on the frozen moat before it gets warm and the boats are put out. I remember once wondering which felt colder—the ducks on the ice or the ducks on the water. I heard that they come down here in the day to escape the duck-hunting, and in the evening fly back to their mountains and lakes."

"I didn't know that."

"I've seen red flags on May Day fluttering down the street where the streetcars run. The ginkgo trees along the road were all decked out in new leaves. It was beautiful—seeing the parade of scarlet banners through the leaves."

The moat below the spot where they were sitting had been filled in as an evening practice-ground for golfers. Beyond this, ginkgo trees, their black trunks silhouetted against the tender leaves, lined the road where streetcars passed to and fro. A pink mist began to veil the evening sky above the trees. Mizuno covered Machie's hand with both his own while she stroked the dog in his lap.

"While I was waiting for you, Machie, the tune of some quiet accordian song came into my head. I was lying down with my eyes closed."

"What sort of song?"

"Well, like 'Kimigayo'. . ."

"The National Anthem?" Surprised, Machie drew closer to Mizuno. "But you didn't enlist, did you?"

"I hear it over the radio late every night."

"Then it must be at about the same time that I say 'Good night' to you."

Machie didn't tell Mizuno about Gimpei. Indeed, she had already forgotten the fact that a strange man had spoken to her. She could have seen Gimpei lying in the new grass if she had looked hard enough, but even then she would probably not have recognized him as the man who had spoken to her a little while before. Gimpei, however, couldn't help watching them both. He felt the cold of the earth through his back. It was around the time of year when people would be considering changing from winter to spring coats, but Gimpei had none at all. He rolled over on his side so that he faced Machie and Mizuno. He cursed their happiness more than he envied it. When he shut his eyes he saw the lovers drifting, engulfed in flames, on waves that could not cool them. He took the vision as a sign that their happiness would not last.

"Your mother is beautiful, isn't she, Gin-chan?"

Gimpei heard Yayoi's voice. He was sitting beside her under the wild cherry trees in blossom by the lakeshore. The flowers were reflected in the water and the birds sang.

"I like the way your mother's teeth show when she talks."

Perhaps Yayoi was wondering how such a beautiful person had come to marry a man as ugly as his father.

"My father has no other brothers or sisters—only your mother. He often says your mother should come back with you to our home now that your father's dead."

"No, I wouldn't like that," Gimpei said and blushed.

Had he said that he disliked the idea because he was

92

frightened of losing his mother, or was he shy at the happy prospect of living in the same house as Yayoi? Perhaps both.

In those days Gimpei's household included his grandparents and his father's divorced elder sister, as well as his mother. Gimpei's father had died in the lake when Gimpei was ten, and as he had had head injuries people said that he had been murdered and his body thrown into the lake. But he had had water in his lungs, so it was possible that he had drowned. Nevertheless there was a rumor that he had quarreled with someone and been pushed into the lake. Yayoi's family bitterly resented his father's death, thinking that he had killed himself just to spite them—in his wife's village of all places. At ten, Gimpei had resolved that the murderer, if there was one, would never go undiscovered. When he visited his mother's village he used to hide in a thicket near the spot where his father's corpse had been recovered and watch the passers-by. He reasoned that the murderer would be unable to pass there without showing some sign of guilt. On one occasion a man had come along with a cow, and when the animal had started to go wild at the crucial spot, Gimpei had almost choked with excitement. He also remembered there was a bush with white flowers which he picked and took home to press in a book, vowing to avenge his father's murder.

"My mother wouldn't want to go back either, since

93

my father was murdered in this village," Gimpei said.

Yayoi was surprised at the deathly pallor of Gimpei's face.

Yayoi hadn't told him of the rumor in the village that his father's ghost now haunted the shores of the lake. The villagers claimed that the sound of footsteps followed those who went near the spot where he had perished, but whenever they looked round, there was nobody behind them. When they ran away, the footsteps would recede, for the ghost was unable to run after them.

Even the song of a bird gradually descending from the upper to the lower branches of a cherry tree reminded Yayoi of the ghost's footsteps, and she said, "Let's go home, Gin-chan. The flowers reflected in the lake, they kind of scare me."

"They're not scaring."

"That's because you don't look at them closely."

"They're pretty, though, aren't they?"

As Yayoi stood up, Gimpei jerked her hand toward him, and she fell down on top of him.

Yayoi shouted "Gin-chan!" and ran off, the skirt of her kimono flapping open. Gimpei chased after her. She stopped, panting for breath, and clung to Gimpei's shoulders.

"Gin-chan, come and stay at our place with your mother."

"No, I don't want to," Gimpei said, holding Yayoi

94

firmly in his arms, and burst into tears. Yayoi stared at him in blank astonishment.

"Your mother told my father that she would never survive in a home like yours," Yayoi said after a while.

It was the only time Gimpei put his arms around Yayoi.

Yayoi's house on the lake, where his mother had been born, was quite well-to-do, and it was only some years later, when Gimpei's mother had returned to her parents' home and he was a struggling student in Tokyo, that Gimpei came to suspect that something odd must have happened for his mother to have married out of her class. While he was in Tokyo, his mother died of tuberculosis, and his small allowance was cut off. Then his grandfather died, and this left only an aunt and grandmother alive in Gimpei's family. He had heard that his aunt had brought back with her a daughter by her former husband, but as he hadn't written home for years he didn't know whether she had found a husband for the girl.

Gimpei felt there wasn't much difference between lying in the new grass after following Machie and hiding in the thicket by the lake in Yayoi's village. The same sadness flowed through his body, but he no longer thought seriously of avenging his father. Even if there had been a murderer, he must be old by now. If some ugly old man sought him out and confessed the murder, would he feel relieved, as if some evil spirit had departed from his soul? Would he regain his youth and become like those two lying over there? The reflection of wild cherry blossoms in the lake floated across his mind. The lake lay like a wide mirror, without a ripple on its surface. Gimpei closed his eyes and remembered his mother's face.

When Gimpei opened his eyes, he saw the student standing alone on the bank. The girl and her dog seemed to have left, and Gimpei sprang to his feet, eager not to miss seeing her go down the slope. Dusk had settled on the leaves of the ginkgo trees, and though the road was deserted the girl did not look back. The dog was hurrying home ahead of her, pulling the leash taut. The girl walked beautifully with short, quick steps. Gimpei began to whistle, knowing she would return to the slope the following evening, and started walking toward Mizuno. He went on whistling even when Mizuno noticed him.

"Having a good time, are you?" Gimpei said.

Mizuno looked away.

"I said, are you having a good time? Didn't you hear me?"

Mizuno frowned at Gimpei.

"Don't look so put out. Let's sit down and talk. I'm just someone who feels jealous of people who look happy, that's all."

Mizuno turned his back and started to leave.

"Hey! You don't have to run away! I said, let's talk, didn't I?" Gimpei shouted. Mizuno turned around.

"I'm not running away. I don't have anything to say to you."

"What's wrong? Do you think I'm going to blackmail you or something? Let's sit down."

Mizuno remained standing.

"I thought your girl was fantastic. I know you don't like me saying so, but she's really beautiful, isn't she? You must be very happy."

"What of it?"

"I just wanted to talk to someone who's happy. To tell you the truth, she's so beautiful I've been following her all afternoon. I was surprised to find she had a date with you."

Mizuno looked in astonishment at Gimpei, but started to walk away.

"Look, let's have a talk," Gimpei said at once, putting his hand on Mizuno's shoulder from behind. Mizuno thrust him brutally away.

"You fool!"

Gimpei tumbled down the bank onto the asphalt road below and hurt his right shoulder. For a while he sat cross-legged on the road, then stood up holding his shoulder. When he climbed the bank again his assailant had disappeared. Gasping for breath and feeling a heaviness in his chest, Gimpei sat down and let his head sink slowly onto his chest.

He couldn't understand why he had gone over to the student and spoken to him after the girl left. He hadn't really had any malicious intention in mind when he approached the boy, whistling. Perhaps he had simply wanted to talk to him about the girl's beauty, and if the student had been more receptive, Gimpei might have been able to tell him something about her beauty which the youth had not yet discovered. But it was obviously stupid for him to have spoken so abruptly and unpleasantly. "Having a good time, are you?" He should have put it differently. Gimpei felt tearful when he realized how feeble he had become. To think that one shove from the student had sent him headlong down the bank! As he sat there holding onto the fresh grass with one hand and rubbing his aching shoulder with the other, the pinkish glow of twilight reflected faintly in his narrowed eyes.

The girl would be unlikely to return to the slope with her dog. She might walk up the avenue of ginkgo trees once more, for the student would be unable to get in touch with her until the next day, but now that Gimpei was known to the boy, he could never show himself either on the slope or the bank. He looked around the bank in vain for a hiding place. The image of the girl in her white sweater and red-checked jeans flashed before his eyes. The pink sky seemed to suffuse his brain.

"Hisako! Hisako!" he cried out in a choking voice. It was Hisako Tamaki's name that he called.

Once, when he was riding in a taxi to meet Hisako, the city sky had looked pink though it was long before sunset—only about three o'clock in the afternoon. Through the closed window beside him the sky was tinted a bluish color, but in the driver's lowered window the sky seemed a different shade.

"The sky's slightly pink, isn't it?" Gimpei had asked, leaning toward the driver's shoulder.

"Looks like it."

The driver sounded as if it didn't make much difference what color it was.

"Isn't it tinged with pink? Why, I wonder? You don't think it's just my eyes, do you?"

"No, it isn't your eyes."

As he leant forward, he caught a whiff of the driver's old clothes.

Since then, whenever he rode in a taxi, he couldn't help being conscious of two worlds: one pale pink and the other pale blue. The things he had seen through his window had probably been tinted blue, and what he saw through the driver's lowered window must have looked faintly pink by contrast. That was the simple explanation, but Gimpei was persuaded that the sky, the walls, the roads, and even the trunks of the trees by the roadside really were perhaps this curious pink color. In spring and autumn many taxis have the driver's window open and the back windows closed, and although Gimpei's means did not allow him to take a taxi whenever he went out, each ride added to this feeling.

He became accustomed to the idea that the driver's world was a warm pink and the passenger's a cold blue. And Gimpei was the passenger. Of course, the world looks cleaner through glass; perhaps it was the dust in the air that gave the sky and streets of Tokyo this pinkish tinge.

Leaning forward with his elbows on the back of the driver's seat, Gimpei would survey his pink world and become irritated by the warmth of the stagnant air. "Hey!" he wanted to shout to the driver, and lunge at him. Doubtless it was a sign of a desire to rebel against or challenge something, but if he had clutched at the driver, people would have thought he was mad. Yet since the city and sky normally appeared slightly pink while it was still daylight, no driver ever seemed afraid of him, even when Gimpei thrust his alarming face near.

Indeed, there was no reason to be frightened of Gimpei. He had first noticed these contrasting worlds of pale pink and blue when he was on his way to meet Hisako, and he always leaned toward the driver's back in this way. Since that first time, when the smell of the driver's old clothes had reminded him of Hisako's blue serge uniform, he had always thought of

Hisako in taxis. Her smell returned with every driver; it made no difference if the driver was wearing new clothes.

Around the time that he first discovered the pink-colored sky, Gimpei had been dismissed from his teaching post and Hisako had changed schools, which forced them to meet secretly. He had been afraid of this prospect even before it happened and had once whispered to Hisako, "Be sure never to tell Miss Onda. Never! It's just a secret between the two of us!" Hisako blushed as if they were already meeting in secret.

"A secret, if it's kept, can be sweet and comforting, but once it leaks out it can turn on you with a vengeance."

Hisako, with dimples in her cheeks, raised her eyes and stared hard at Gimpei. They were in a corner of the hall outside the classroom. A girl outside sprang at the branch of a leafy cherry tree near the window and swung there as if on a metal bar. The branch shook so violently that the sound of leaves could be heard through the hall windows.

"Lovers have no other friends. No one at all! Even Miss Onda is an enemy now—the eyes and ears of the outside world!"

"But surely I can tell her?"

"No! You mustn't!" Gimpei looked round in alarm.

"But I feel upset. When she sympathizes and asks

101

me what's wrong, I'm afraid I may not be able to keep the secret."

"Why do you need a friend's sympathy?" Gimpei said in a sharper voice.

"When I see her, I'm sure I'll start crying. After I got home yesterday, my eyes were swollen from crying and I tried bathing them in water. In summer we have ice cubes in the refrigerator and it's no problem, but. . ."

"Don't talk nonsense."

"But I can't bear it. . ."

"Let me see your eyes."

Hisako meekly turned up her eyes. But she was not looking at him. Her gaze suggested that she wanted Gimpei to look into her eyes. He lapsed into silence as he became aware of her body.

Before his relationship with Hisako had developed as far as this, he had thought of tapping Nobuko Onda for information about Hisako's family. After all, Hisako had said she told Onda everything. But there was something about Onda that made it difficult for him to approach her. He was afraid that she would see what was in his heart if he were to inquire about Hisako. Onda was a good student, but very independent.

On one occasion in his class Gimpei had read aloud some passages from *Social Relationships between Men and Women* by Yukichi Fukuzawa. He began with the humorous line, "After two hundred yards or so, the couple may walk side by side." Then he read on: "For instance, it is still possible to encounter the absurd anachronism of parents-in-law finding it inappropriate and offensive for a young wife to express regret at parting from her husband when he is going away, or for a young husband to care tenderly for his sick wife."

Most of the girl students burst out laughing, but Onda did not laugh.

"Miss Onda, you're not laughing, are you?" Gimpei said. Onda did not reply.

"Don't you think it funny, Miss Onda?"

"No, I don't."

"I wonder why you can't join in with all the others, who obviously find it amusing even if you don't."

"I don't want to. There's nothing wrong in laughing with the others, I suppose, but I don't think I have to laugh just to conform, do I?"

"You're quibbling," Gimpei said with a wry face. "Miss Onda says it isn't funny. Do you think it's funny?"

A hush fell over the class. Gimpei continued, "She doesn't find the passages amusing. Yukichi Fukuzawa wrote them in 1896, but reading them now, even after the war, Miss Onda is not amused. Frankly, I find that a bit puzzling."

Suddenly, in the middle of his explanation, Gimpei said crossly, "Have any of you ever seen Miss Onda laugh?"—only to be greeted by lively laughter as they replied:

"Yes, I have."

"So have I."

"Yes, she laughs a lot."

Gimpei later came to think that there was something hidden in Hisako's personality that had drawn Onda to her—the same mysterious charm, perhaps, that had compelled Gimpei to follow her and had made her accept his pursuit. Hisako's womanhood had been awakened as though by a sudden electric shock. When she gave herself to Gimpei, even he had trembled so violently that he wondered later whether other girls were like her.

Hisako could be considered Gimpei's first woman. The days when she had been his pupil, and he had loved her even then, now seemed the happiest period of his life. His childhood crush on his cousin, Yayoi, when his father was still alive, was too childish to be called love, though it had certainly been a pure emotion.

Gimpei could never forget a dream he had had about sea bream. He had been nine or ten at the time, and the dream had provoked a good deal of admiration. He had seen an airship floating high above the sea near his village like a great galleon, and the waves below were an almost inky black. But when he looked more closely, he saw that it was a huge sea bream that had leaped above the waves and risen in the sky. And soon there were others... Everywhere fish were leaping from the waves.

"Wow! What huge bream!" Gimpei had shouted before waking up.

"An auspicious dream, a wonderful dream, Gimpei. It means you'll rise in the world," people told him.

The picturebook Yayoi had given him the day before had had an airship in it, but Gimpei had never seen a real one; and although there were such things in those days, they have probably all gone now that large airplanes have been developed. Gimpei's dream of the airship and the fish had become a part of his past. He had interpreted the dream more as a portent of marriage to Yayoi than of success in life. He had not been successful. There would have been little possibility of it even if he had retained his position in high school as a Japanese teacher. He had neither the strength to leap free from the waves of humanity as the magnificent sea bream had done, nor was he man enough to float there in the air above other heads. He was doomed to sink back into the inky waves. Happiness had come briefly when his secret passion for Hisako had first sprung to life, but the shadow of misfortune fell all too soon. Onda's indictment was severe, as if the secret entrusted to her really had turned on them with a frightening vengeance, just as Gimpei had predicted.

Since that incident in class Gimpei had tried not to look at Hisako, but to his discomfort his eyes would turn of their own accord toward Onda's desk. He asked Onda to meet him once in a corner of the school playground, and tried to entreat and threaten her into keeping the secret. But she condemned Gimpei, not so much out of a sense of justice as from her hatred of him and a strong intuition of his guilt. Gimpei tried to make her understand the precious quality of love.

"You're sordid," Onda said bluntly.

"On the contrary. What could be more sordid than revealing a secret that was given to you, and you only? There must be some poisonous insect, some scorpion, crawling inside you!"

"I haven't told anyone the secret."

But it wasn't long before Onda wrote letters to the principal and to Hisako's father. The writer was anonymous, and the letters ended with the words "from a scorpion."

Gimpei was reduced to meeting Hisako secretly in a place of her choosing. The house that Hisako said her father had bought after the war was in a former suburb, but the prewar uptown residence had been destroyed by fire, and only a partly ruined concrete wall was left standing. Hisako liked to meet Gimpei behind this wall, safe from the eyes of the world. On a large section of the war-torn residential area various houses had been built, leaving only a few empty, damaged lots. The danger and uncanny atmosphere once found in such ruins no longer dwelt there, and the place had been forgotten. The overgrown grass was tall enough to hide both of them. Hisako must have felt a sense of security there, since she was only a schoolgirl and the site had once been her home.

It was difficult for Hisako to write to Gimpei and impossible for him to send a letter or telephone her either at home or at the school. Nor could he ask anyone to carry a letter to her. And so he was almost completely deprived of any means of communication with her. But Hisako would come to read what Gimpei scribbled in chalk on the inside wall of the vacant lot. They had decided to write their messages at the bottom of the high wall where, hidden by the grass, the writing would not be noticed. Naturally nothing complicated could be written, and all he could put there were numbers indicating the time and day he wanted Hisako to meet him. Yet it served as a secret notice board, and sometimes Gimpei would come to read what Hisako had written there. When Hisako decided on the time of their meeting she could use special delivery or send a telegram, but Gimpei had to write the time and day on the wall well in advance and then check to see if Hisako had chalked up her sign of agreement. She was closely watched and hardly able to leave home at night.

Their meeting that day when Gimpei first discovered the two worlds of pink and blue in the taxi had been arranged by Hisako. She was waiting, crouched in the grass by the wall. He had said to her once, "Judging from the height of this wall, your father must be very old-fashioned and unfriendly. I imagine there were pieces of broken glass and upturned nails planted on top, too." It was impossible to see over the wall from the new one-storied houses that surrounded it. The only two-storied Western house was so low, perhaps a new style, that even if one were to lean out of the second floor, a third of the garden would be hidden from view. Aware of this, Hisako was on the side near the wall. There was no gate. Perhaps it had been made of wood and had burned down. As the lot was not up for sale, no one was likely to come by out of curiosity, and Gimpei and Hisako could meet there secretly even at three in the afternoon.

"So you're on your way home from school, are you?" Gimpei squatted down with his hand on her head and drew her toward him, taking her pale cheeks between his hands.

"We haven't long. They check the time I leave school every day."

"I know."

"Even though I tell them that I have to stay for a lecture after school on the *Tale of Heike*, my family won't let me go."

"Really? Have you been waiting long? Your legs

108

must be numb." Gimpei lifted her into his lap. Hisako, shy in broad daylight, slid down again.

"This is for you. . ."

"What? Money? How did you get it?"

"I stole it for you," Hisako said, and her eyes gleamed. "Twenty-seven thousand yen."

"Your father's money?"

"I found it in my mother's room."

"I don't need it. Put it back or you'll be found out."

"If they caught me, I could set fire to the house. I wouldn't mind doing it."

"Don't be crazy. Who'd burn down a house worth ten million yen for the sake of twenty-seven thousand?"

"Mother can't make a fuss about it since she seems to have hidden it from Father. I only took it after careful thought, you know. I'm more afraid to put it back where I stole it from. I'm sure I'd start trembling and get caught."

It was not the first time Hisako had given Gimpei money she had stolen. He hadn't suggested it; it was she who had taken the initiative.

"But I can support myself. I have a friend from university who's secretary to a company president called Arita. He sometimes gives me the president's speeches to write."

"Arita? What's his first name?"

"He's an old man called Otoji Arita."

109

"Goodness! He's the chairman of the board of governors at my new school. My father asked Mr. Arita to have me transferred to the school."

"Oh, really?"

"You've been writing the speeches given by the chairman of the board and I didn't know!"

"That's life, isn't it?"

"Yes, I suppose so. You know, sometimes on bright moonlit nights, gazing at the moon, I imagine you're watching too. . . . And when it's wet and windy, I worry about you all alone in your apartment."

"According to what the secretary told me, old Arita has some strange sort of phobia. The secretary asked me to use words like 'wife' and 'marriage' as little as possible in the drafts. He must have expected words like these to crop up in a speech to a girls' school. Did the chairman seem neurotic when he gave the talk?"

"No, I didn't notice."

"I suppose not. Well, not in public," Gimpei nodded to himself.

"Neurotic. What do you mean?"

"There are all kinds of neurotics. Maybe we're neurotic, too. Shall I show you?" Gimpei said. Searching for Hisako's breasts, Gimpei closed his eyes, and a wheatfield near his home arose in his mind. A woman, sitting bareback on a farmer's horse, rode along the path across the wheatfield. The woman had a white towel, knotted in the front, around her neck.

"You could throttle me. . . I don't want to go home," Hisako whispered passionately. Gimpei was surprised to find himself grasping her neck with the fingers of one hand. He put the other hand round to measure her neck. It was soft; his fingertips touched in a circle around it. Gimpei slipped the bundle of money into Hisako's dress. She drew back, her breasts tightening.

"Be a good girl and take the money home. . . I'm afraid either you or I will end up committing a crime if we do this sort of thing. Didn't Onda accuse me of being a criminal? She wrote in her letter that I told so many lies and had such an air of gloom about me that she was sure I'd done something seriously wrong. Didn't you know that? Have you seen her recently?"

"No, I haven't. I haven't had a letter from her either. I don't even like her."

Gimpei remained silent for a while. Hisako spread out a square piece of nylon for Gimpei to sit on. He felt the coldness of the earth through it, and there was a smell of dank grass and weeds.

"I wish you would follow me again. Follow me without my knowing. I want you to do that once more on my way home from school. My new school is farther away, you know."

"And you'll pretend to notice me for the first time in front of that splendid gate, won't you! You'll stare

111

at me and blush from the other side of the iron gate!"

"No. I'll ask you to come in! My house is so big that you won't be found. I'm certain of it. Even my room has enough space to hide you in."

Gimpei felt a flame of happiness rise in him. And not long afterward he put her idea into practice, only to be discovered by Hisako's family.

Since then the months and the years had forced a distance between him and Hisako. Yet now, as he lay watching the faint blush of twilight after the student had pushed him down the bank, it was Hisako's name that escaped his lips. "Hisako, Hisako," he called pathetically. When he returned to his apartment, he discovered that his shoulders and kneecaps had turned purple: the bank had been about twice his own height.

The following evening Gimpei felt compelled to see the girl again on the slope lined with ginkgo trees. She had been almost undisturbed by his pursuit; how could he possibly harm her, Gimpei thought to himself sorrowfully. It was like grieving after the flight of a wild goose through the sky . . . or watching the shining stream of time flow past. His own life might end tomorrow, and even the girl would not be beautiful forever.

But since Gimpei had made himself known to the student by talking with him the previous day, he couldn't loiter on the slope under the ginkgo trees, nor could he stay on the bank where the boy would be waiting for her. He decided to hide in the ditch between the tree-lined sidewalk and the aristocrat's mansion. If he were questioned by a policeman he could say that his legs hurt and that he was drunk and had fallen in the ditch, or that he had been thrown into it by a hoodlum. As drunkenness seemed the safer explanation, Gimpei had one drink before leaving home to make his breath smell of liquor.

Gimpei had seen the ditch the day before and thought it was deep, but when he got in he found it was wide but quite shallow, with both sides lined with good solid walls and the bottom also paved with stone. Grass grew in the crevices between the stones, and last year's decaying leaves lay matted on the floor. If he pressed himself close against the wall on the side of the road he wouldn't be seen by passers-by coming up the straight slope. He hid there for twenty or thirty minutes, conscious of a desire to gnaw at one of the stones in the wall. He noticed a violet flowering between the stones and, creeping closer, he opened his mouth, bit it off with his teeth and swallowed it. It was difficult to swallow, and with a moan Gimpei struggled to hold back his tears.

The girl appeared at the foot of the slope with her dog. Spreading out his arms and gripping the edges of the stones, Gimpei gradually raised his head. He felt that the wall was about to crumble; his hands were

113

trembling and his heart thumped against the stones.

The girl was in the white sweater she had worn the day before, but she was wearing a dark red skirt instead of jeans and her shoes were better too. The white and ruby colors approached, floating amid the fresh green trees. When she passed just above Gimpei's head her hand was in front of his eyes. The skin was fair, and on her arm more delicate still. Staring up at her lovely chin, Gimpei closed his eyes with a cry of admiration. Then, seeing the boy, he muttered aloud, "Ah, there he is."

The student was waiting for her at the top of the bank. As Gimpei watched from the bottom of the ditch about halfway down the slope, the two walked away across the bank, seeming to glide over the green grass that hid their knees. Gimpei waited until dark for the girl to return, but she did not come down the slope. Perhaps the student had talked to her about the strange man he had seen yesterday and they had avoided the road.

Since then Gimpei often wandered along the slope with the ginkgo trees and lingered on the grassy bank for hours, but he did not find the girl. A vision of her had even drawn him out at night. The young leaves had grown quickly to a vigorous green, and the dark overhanging trees cast menacing shadows in the moonlight across the asphalt road. He remembered the day when, gripped by a sudden fear of the blackness of the

114

ocean, he had scurried home to his village on the coast of the Japan Sea. He heard the sound of kittens mewing at the bottom of the ditch and stopped to look down. He couldn't see them, but a box was faintly visible, with something moving inside. "It's certainly a good place to dump kittens," he thought to himself.

Someone had abandoned the newborn kittens in the box. How many of them were there? Poor things, they would die of hunger. He tried to identify with the kittens and stayed on to listen to their wailing. After that evening, however, the girl never reappeared on the slope.

It was in early June that he read in the newspaper about a firefly-catching party to be held on the moat not far from the slope. It was the moat where there were boats for hire. Gimpei was sure the girl would come. Her house must be nearby, for she had taken her dog for walks there.

The lake in his mother's village was also famous for fireflies, and Gimpei used to be taken there by her to catch them. When he went to bed he released them in his mosquito net, and Yayoi followed suit. With the sliding doors wide open, he could see her inside her net in the next room, counting the fireflies to see who had caught the most. They were difficult to count as they flitted about.

"Gin-chan, you cheat! You're always cheating!"

Yayoi got up and brandished a fist at him.

When she started to beat the net with her hands, it swayed, stirring up the fireflies that had settled on it; but since the net offered no resistance, Yayoi grew more excited and sprang up and down as she swung her fists about. She was in her summer kimono with short narrow sleeves, and the skirt was gathered up higher than her knees, making the base of the mosquito net billow out strangely toward Gimpei. Yayoi looked like a ghost with a blue mosquito net over her head.

"Now you've got more than I have! Look behind you!" Gimpei said, and Yayoi turned around.

"Of course I have!"

She certainly seemed to have collected more than Gimpei. The net swung to and fro with its cargo of flickering lights.

Gimpei could still remember that Yayoi's kimono had had a splashed pattern of large crosses that evening. But what was his mother, who was inside his net, doing? Hadn't she said anything about Yayoi creating such a disturbance? And hadn't Yayoi's mother, who was sleeping with her, told her off? Her little brother must have been with them too. Yet Yayoi's was the only presence he could recall.

Even now a vision sometimes came to him of lightning at night over the lake near his mother's village. The entire surface was illuminated in those brief seconds of light, and fireflies could be seen on the shore in the ensuing darkness. Their appearance could possibly have been a genuine part of the vision, but he suspected they were an afterthought, since lightning generally occurs in summer when fireflies are about. Though he made no effort to identify the fireflies with the spirit of his dead father, whom they had found in the lake, he felt there was something sinister about that moment of sudden darkness when the lightning vanished from the lake. He knew it was only a vision, yet whenever he saw that vast and deep expanse of motionless water lit suddenly by the night sky, he felt crushed by the awful mystery of nature, the agony of time. It was as if he himself had been struck by lightning and everything around him had burst with light.

His first electrifying contact with Hisako had been the same. Once rigid and inexperienced, she had been transformed. Even Gimpei had been surprised at how forward she had suddenly become, and it was with some similar feeling that he found her leading him into her parents' house and creeping into her bedroom.

"It really is a big house, isn't it? I don't know how I'll get out without being seen."

"I'll show you the way out. You can climb out of the window."

"But this is upstairs, isn't it?" Gimpei winced.

"I'll make a rope by joining some sashes together or something. You'll see."

"You don't keep a dog, do you? I'm afraid I don't like them."

"No, we don't have a dog."

Instead of continuing, Hisako turned and looked at Gimpei with shining eyes. "You know I can't marry you, but I wanted to be alone with you in my room just once. I hate all this secrecy, forever 'hidden in the grass.'"

"The expression 'hidden in the grass' can of course have its literal meaning, but nowadays it usually means 'under the sod' or 'in the grave.'"

"Oh, really?" Hisako wasn't paying attention.

"Anyway, none of that matters now that I'm no longer a Japanese teacher."

The trouble was, however, that he had been that kind of teacher in the past. A terrible society, Gimpei thought, and overwhelmed by the splendor and unexpected luxury of a schoolgirl's Western-style room, he felt no better than a criminal on the run. His mood had changed since he had followed Hisako from the entrance of her new school to the gate of her house. This second pursuit had been nothing but a game, where Hisako knew all the rules and only pretended to be innocent. Yet, though she had long since given in to him, he was pleased that she had initiated the scheme.

"Please wait a minute," Hisako said, squeezing his hand. "It's suppertime."

He drew her toward him and kissed her. She wanted a long kiss and rested her whole weight in Gimpei's arms. He had to support her, and this made him a little happier.

"What do you want to do in the meantime?"

"Well . . . have you got a photograph album or something?"

"No, not even a diary, I'm afraid." Hisako shook her head, looking up into his eyes.

"You never talk about your childhood, do you? Why?"

"It's not very interesting."

Hisako left without wiping her lips. He wondered how she would look sitting at the supper table with her family. Behind a curtain drawn over an alcove in the wall, Gimpei discovered a small washbasin. He turned the water on cautiously, then washed his face and hands and rinsed his mouth. He even wanted to take his socks off to wash his feet, but he couldn't bring himself to put them in the same basin that Hisako washed her face in. Anyway, cleaning his feet wouldn't make them look any better; it would only confirm how ugly they were.

Their secret meeting would never have been discovered if Hisako had not made sandwiches and carried them up to him. It was reckless, too, to have brought him coffee on a silver tray. Soon they heard someone knocking on the door and Hisako, who must

119

have come to a sudden decision, said in an accusing tone: "Is that you, Mother?"

"Yes."

"Please don't open the door. I've a visitor."

"Who is it?"

"It's my teacher," Hisako answered candidly in a low, steady voice. At that moment Gimpei stood up, bathed in a wild glow of happiness. If he had had a pistol with him he would have shot Hisako from behind. He could see the scene: the bullet passed through her breast and hit her mother behind the door. Both women, standing with the door between them, threw themselves backward, but Hisako turned, arching her body in a graceful curve, and clutched at Gimpei's legs as she fell. Blood gushed from her wound and, flowing down his legs, soaked the inside of his feet. In an instant, the coarse, blackish skin had become as soft and pure as rose petals, his wrinkled arches as smooth as mother-of-pearl. And bathed in Hisako's warm blood, even his crooked, gnarled and shriveled toes, which were as long as a monkey's, became as graceful as a mannequin's. The sudden thought that so much blood could never have come from Hisako alone made Gimpei aware of the wound in his own chest. He felt faint, as if wrapped in the five-colored clouds on which Amida Buddha rides to receive the spirits of true believers. This exquisite fantasy lasted only an instant.

"My daughter's blood is mixed in the ointment she took to school for your athlete's foot."

Gimpei heard the voice of Hisako's father and immediately stiffened. But he was hallucinating again. When he came to his senses, only the figure of Hisako calmly facing the door emerged, and his fear abated. There was no noise from the other side. He felt he could see the mother through the door, trembling before her daughter's stare; she was a hen, stark naked, her feathers plucked out by her own chick. Her forlorn footsteps disappeared down the hall. Going straight up to the door, Hisako locked it firmly and turned toward Gimpei, her hand on the handle. As she stood with her back against the door, tears streamed down her cheeks.

Inevitably they soon heard her father's rough steps approaching.

"Here! Open the door, Hisako! Open it at once, will you?" Her father rattled the handle.

"All right, I'll see your father," Gimpei said.

"No, I don't want you to."

"Why not? I can't do anything else."

"I don't want you to see my father."

"I won't be violent. I haven't got a gun."

"I don't want you to. Get out through the window. Please!"

"The window? Okay. It should be easy with feet like mine."

"It's dangerous with shoes on."

"I don't have them on."

Hisako took two or three sashes out of a chest-of-drawers and tied them together. Outside the door her father grew more and more enraged.

"I'll open it in a second. Just wait a moment, please. We're not going to commit double suicide or anything."

"What? What a terrible thing to say!"

But the words seemed to have taken her father unawares, and for a while they heard nothing more from outside the door.

Hisako wept as she strained to take Gimpei's weight on the sashes which hung from the window. She had fastened them around both hands, and Gimpei brushed the tip of his nose against her fingers before beginning to climb smoothly down. He had wanted to kiss her fingers, but as he was looking down, he touched them with his nose. Hisako braced herself with her elbows squared against the wall below the window, straightening her back. Hanging outside the window Gimpei was unable to reach up and give her a grateful parting kiss, but when his feet touched the ground, he tugged at the sashes twice with emotion. The second pull received no response, and the sashes fluttered down from the lighted window.

"Are they for me?" he called. "Then I'll keep them forever."

Gimpei ran off through the garden, swinging the

sashes round one arm as he went. Glancing back quickly, he saw Hisako and another figure—probably her father—standing side by side at the window he had escaped from. The father seemed unable to raise his voice, and Gimpei sprang like a monkey over the ornamental iron gate.

Was Hisako now married, he wondered, after all that had happened? . . .

Since that day, Gimpei met her only once more. Of course he had often gone to the place Hisako had described as "hidden in the grass"—the wartime ruin of her family's old home—but he found neither Hisako crouching there in the grass nor any message written on the inside of the concrete wall. Yet he never abandoned hope and continued to return to the spot occasionally, even in winter when the grass was withered and covered with snow. Then, one day in spring, he was astonished to find Hisako sitting there amid the fresh green grass.

She was with Nobuko Onda. At first Gimpei's heart leapt at the thought that she had perhaps come here sometimes in the hope of seeing him and had simply missed meeting him. The look of amazement on her face, however, told him that she hadn't expected Gimpei at all and had only arranged to meet Onda there. But why Onda, of all people? And in their old secret place? After all, she had betrayed them. Gimpei decided to be careful what he said.

123

"Sir!" Hisako called.

"Sir!" echoed Onda in a louder voice as though to keep her in check.

"Are you still going around with this sort of person, Miss Tamaki?" Gimpei jerked his chin in Onda's direction. The two girls were sitting on a thin, square piece of nylon.

"Hisako went to her school graduation ceremony today, Mr. Momoi," Onda proclaimed, staring up at Gimpei.

"Oh! Her graduation ceremony. . . I didn't know." He had already said more than he had wanted to.

"I haven't been to school since that day," Hisako said in a pleading voice.

"I see."

Her words moved him deeply, but whether he was conscious of Onda's hostile presence or simply betrayed by his former position as a teacher, he said unexpectedly, "But how could you graduate if that's so?"

"Of course she could. The chairman of the board recommended her." The answer came from Onda. It wasn't clear whether she meant good or ill toward Hisako.

"Look, I know you're a clever girl, Miss Onda, but stop butting in, will you?" Gimpei said. "Did the chairman of the board give a speech at the ceremony?" he asked Hisako.

"Yes."

"I no longer write the drafts for old Arita's speeches, you know. I suppose the speech today sounded different from the earlier ones."

"It was short."

"What in heaven's name are you two talking about?" Onda interrupted. "I thought you'd have more than this to say to each other, even if you did meet accidentally."

"If you'd just leave us alone, we'd have a great deal to talk about. But not with a spy like you listening in. If you have anything to say to Miss Tamaki, say it quickly."

"I'm not a spy. I just wanted to protect Miss Tamaki from your bad influence. It was my letter that enabled her to change schools, and though she didn't attend her new one, she was at least rid of your poisonous presence. I'm very fond of Miss Tamaki, and whatever you try and do to me I'll fight back. Anyway, I'm sure she loathes you."

"What am I to do with you? If you don't get out of here quickly you're liable to get hurt."

"I won't leave Miss Tamaki. I'm the one who arranged to meet her. So go away please."

"Are you some sort of chaperone?"

"Why should I be? You're horrible." Onda looked aside. "Hisako, let's go home. Tell this awful man that you hate him and never want to see him again."

"Here! I haven't finished that talk you said I should have with Miss Tamaki. So you go away." And he patted Onda condescendingly on the head.

"This is awful," Onda said, shaking her head.

"It certainly is. When did you last wash your hair? You'd better do something about it before it starts to smell. No other man would touch hair like this." Onda looked furious. "There, there, why don't you run along? I'm not above hitting or kicking a woman, you know."

"And I don't mind being hit or kicked."

"Very well." Gimpei was about to pull Onda away by the wrist when he turned to Hisako and said, "Okay?"

Hisako's eyes seemed to show assent, so Gimpei, encouraged, dragged Onda away.

"No! Stop! What do you think you're doing?"

She tried to bite Gimpei's hand.

"So you want to kiss my awful little hand, do you?"

"I'll bite you," Onda yelled, but she didn't carry out her threat.

When they reached the spot where the gate had once stood, on the other side of the ruins, Onda stood up straight to avoid drawing attention to herself. Gimpei, however, held onto her wrist and hailed an empty taxi.

"Look, this girl has run away from home, and there's someone from her family waiting for her in front of

Omori Station. Could you get her over there in a hurry?" Gimpei lifted the girl up and bundled her into the taxi. He took a one-thousand-yen note out of his pocket and threw it onto the driver's seat. The taxi moved off.

When he returned, he found Hisako still sitting behind the wall on the piece of nylon.

"I pushed her into a taxi, explaining that she had run away from home. She's gone to Omori. It cost me a thousand yen."

"I'm sure she'll get her revenge by writing to my family again."

"Another letter from a scorpion, eh?"

"But she may not. She wants to go to university, and came here to persuade me to try as well. Her plan is to become some sort of private tutor to me, so that my father will pay her college fees. Her family isn't very well off."

"Did she really meet you here to discuss this?"

"Yes. She's often written to me since January and asked me to meet her. But as I didn't want her to come to my house, I wrote and told her I'd be able to get out for the graduation ceremony. She met me at the school gate, and I wanted to come here once more anyway."

"I don't know how often I've been here since that day . . . even once when the snow was deep. . ."

Hisako nodded, showing her lovely dimples. To

look at this girl, who would have imagined that she had had an affair with Gimpei? What effects of his "poisonous presence" could be seen in her, Gimpei wondered.

"I've often thought that you might have come here," said Hisako.

"You know, there was snow here long after it had gone from the streets. I suppose it's because the wall is high. Anyway people shoveled snow over here from outside. There was a mountain of it this side of the gate, and somehow that too seemed to stand in the way of our love. . . I thought there might be a baby buried under it. . ."

Surprised at the strange and incoherent statements he was making, Gimpei abruptly fell silent. But Hisako nodded serenely. He hurriedly changed the subject.

"And are you going to university with Miss Onda? What are you going to study?"

"There's not much point in a girl going to university," Hisako answered indifferently.

"The sashes that day—do you remember? I've treasured them ever since. You gave them to me to remember you by, didn't you?"

"I'm afraid they just slipped out of my hands," Hisako said innocently.

"Did your father shout at you?"

"He doesn't let me out alone."

"If I'd known that you never went back to school,

then I'd have climbed up to your window in the night."

"Sometimes I used to stand at the window at midnight and look out into the garden," Hisako replied. But during the time she had been forbidden to go out alone, Hisako seemed to have reverted to her former innocence, and Gimpei's spirits sagged as he realized he could no longer fathom her thoughts. Yet when he sat down on the other half of the nylon cloth where Onda had been, Hisako did not avoid him. She was wearing a beautiful, new, blue dress with lace trimmings at the collar. It must have been for the graduation ceremony. It also occurred to Gimpei that she might be wearing the latest makeup, so natural that he couldn't detect it. There was a faint fragrance about her. He put his hand gently on her shoulder.

"Let's go somewhere. Let's run away together—far away. To the lonely shores of a lake. . ."

"I've made up my mind not to meet you again. I'm happy to have seen you here today, but please make this our last meeting." Hisako spoke in a calm and appealing voice that betrayed no sign of rejecting him. "If I can't exist without seeing you, I'll look for you whatever happens."

"But I'm sinking to the bottom of the world. . ."

"I'll find you—even underground, in the passages below Ueno Station."

"Let's go now!"

"No, not now,"

"Why not?"

"I've been hurt and still feel the pain. But if I still need you when I'm better, then I'll come."

"I wonder. . ."

Gimpei felt a numbness in him spreading right down to his feet.

"I understand. I don't want to drag you down into my world. . . But be sure to bury deep the things that I've drawn out in you. . . They might be dangerous. I'll always be grateful to you. I'll cherish your memory all my life, in a world quite different from yours."

"I shall try to forget you, if I can."

"Yes, that would be better." Though Gimpei said it forcefully, he felt a piercing sadness. "But today. . ." His voice trembled.

Unexpectedly, Hisako nodded.

She remained silent in the taxi and, regaining her composure, sat there with her eyes tight shut and a light flush on her cheeks.

"Open your eyes. I bet there's a devil in there."

Hisako promptly opened them wide, but there was nothing haunting them.

"Sad, aren't they?" he said and took her eyelid between his lips. "Do you remember?"

"Yes, I remember." Hisako's whisper sounded hollow, the faintest murmur in Gimpei's ear.

Since then he had not seen her again. He often

130

wandered out to the ruined lot, and one day found that the area round the gate had been boarded up, the grass cut down and the ground leveled. Eighteen months, perhaps two years later, construction work had begun on what looked like a small house. It couldn't be for Hisako's father. Gimpei wondered if he had sold the lot. He stood with eyes closed, listening to the confident rhythm of the carpenter's plane.

"Goodbye," he said to an absent Hisako. He hoped that his memory of her here would make those who were to live in the new house happy. The sound of the plane was very satisfying.

Gimpei eventually stopped coming to this place that had once been "hidden in the grass." It appeared to have passed to another owner, but Gimpei had no way of knowing that Hisako had married and that it was she who was about to move into the house.

"I'm sure she'll come," Gimpei said to himself. He was so confident that Machie would come to catch fireflies down by the moat where the boats were for hire that he did eventually meet her a third time.

The event was spread over about five days, but though he was prepared to go there every day, he had already singled out one night for her visit. Two days after it began the newspaper carried a report on it, so it was perhaps not instinct alone that prompted Gimpei's choice, for the girl might have read the article and been encouraged to go along. When Gimpei left home with the paper in his pocket, his heart was full of happy anticipation at the prospect of meeting her. Words seemed inadequate to describe the intensity of her long, tapering eyes, and as he walked along he traced the shape of a tiny, beautiful fish around his own eyes with his thumb and forefinger. Heavenly music filled his ears.

Adoringly, Gimpei said to himself, "In my next life I shall be born with beautiful feet. You will be just as you are now, and we'll dance together in a ballet of white." The girl's dress was the white tutu of classical

132

ballet, and the skirt swirled and fluttered.

"Isn't she beautiful? I'm sure she comes from a good family. Unfortunately such perfection doesn't last after the age of sixteen or seventeen, and even she will only be at her best for a few brief years," Gimpei thought. But what made her beauty so pure and radiant, when every other girl seemed to bury her youth and looks in the dust of school textbooks?

There was a notice on the boathouse: "Fireflies will be released at eight o'clock." In Tokyo it gets dark at around half past seven in June, so until then Gimpei strolled back and forth across the bridge over the moat.

"Will those who want boats please take a number and wait!" a megaphone announced repeatedly. The firefly-catching had attracted such crowds that it seemed to have been deliberately thought up by the man who hired out boats. As they waited, the crowds on the bridge had little else to do but look down aimlessly at people getting in and out of boats or watch the boats on the water. But none of this claimed Gimpei's attention. It was the girl that he was looking for.

He had already been twice to the slope where the ginkgo trees were. He squatted down for a while with his hands against the stone wall, thinking he might hide in the ditch, just as he had done before. But the evening's event had drawn other people there, and their footsteps made him hurry down. He heard more steps behind him, but didn't look round.

133

Coming to the crossroads at the foot of the slope, Gimpei surveyed the din and bustle of the scene. The lights on the roads beyond the bridge lit up the low night sky, and the headlamps of cars flickered about on the streets. Gimpei felt excited now that it was about to begin, but for some reason he could not turn toward the moat and crossed over to the other side. It was a residential district. The sound of footsteps behind him receded as they turned toward the firefly-catching, but suddenly Gimpei felt someone stick a sheet of paper on his back. There was a red arrow drawn on jet black paper, and the arrow pointed in the direction of the event. Gimpei struggled to snatch the paper off his back, but was unable to reach it. Pain shot through his arm and the joint creaked.

"You can't follow the arrow if it's on your back, can you? I'll take it off for you."

At the sound of a woman's soothing voice, Gimpei looked round. There was no one behind him, though people were approaching from the residential district on their way to the moat. The voice had come from a radio and seemed to be part of some incidental dialogue in a radio play.

"Thank you!" Gimpei waved his hand to the hallucinatory voice and walked on with lighter steps, buoyed up by the thought that odd moments of release came in any man's life.

Along the approach to the bridge stood some stalls

with fireflies for sale at five yen each and forty yen for a cage. There were no fireflies over the moat. When he reached the middle of the bridge, Gimpei noticed a huge cage of fireflies on a low tower built into the water.

"Set them free! Set them free!" children were yelling eagerly. Apparently the fireflies were to be scattered from the tower and caught by the crowds below. Two or three men were up on the tower, and a mass of small boats were jammed around its base. A number of people in the boats carried bamboo branches and nets, and more bristled from the crowds on the bridge and near the water's edge. Some of the poles were very long.

At the end of the bridge were more stalls selling fireflies. Gimpei heard someone say, "They sell Okayama fireflies over there, and Koshu fireflies on this side. The Okayama ones are smaller, really tiny and quite different." He went toward the stalls and found that the fireflies there cost ten yen each, twice as much, but seven fireflies with a cage sold for the special price of a hundred yen.

"Give me ten big ones," he said and handed over two hundred yen.

"All these ones are big. Ten besides the seven?"

When the firefly seller pushed his arm into the large, wet, cotton bag, dull lights pulsated inside as though breathing. The man picked out one or two fireflies at a time and transferred them to a long, pipe-shaped cage. When Gimpei held it up to his eyes, thinking there could never be as many as seventeen fireflies in the cage, the man blew into it and the insects glowed. Some of the man's spit sprayed into Gimpei's face.

"I think it needs another ten to cheer it up a bit."

While the man was counting out ten more, there was a shriek of joy from the children, and Gimpei was suddenly showered with water. The fireflies released from the tower flew up into the sky, then dropped feebly earthward like spent fireworks. Those that flew close to the surface of the water and could barely glide off again were scooped up in the nets and bamboo branches of the boats. There were probably fewer than ten fireflies released, but the scramble to catch them created such a commotion that the nets and branches were soon soaked, and as everyone waved their wet branches about they splashed water on the people standing on the shore.

"They're not flying well this year, are they? It must be the cold weather," someone said. It seemed to be an annual event.

But no more fireflies were set free, though everyone waited expectantly for them.

An announcement was made from the boathouse on the opposite shore: "The fireflies will be released until about nine o'clock." The men on the tower did not move, and the crowd waited quietly below. The sound of oars could be heard as parties in boats, not much concerned about the fireflies, rowed across the water.

"I hope they'll free them soon!"

"They don't want to. They have to spin it out a bit."

Adults were talking. Satisfied with his purchase, Gimpei stepped back from the water's edge to avoid being splashed again. Carrying his cage of twenty-seven fireflies, he went and leaned against a tree in front of a police box. He could scan the area more easily away from the crowd like this and, besides, he felt strangely peaceful next to the young policeman who stood looking toward the moat with a detached and gentle expression on his face. As long as he stayed there, he couldn't fail to see the girl.

Before long the fireflies were being released continuously from the top of the tower. "Continuously" was not really the right word, for the men who were gathering a handful of fireflies at a time before tossing them out had trouble catching them—or perhaps deliberately calculated the timing—so that the crowd's excitement would surge up, ebb again, then rise still higher. Gimpei found it hard to remain as calm as the policeman standing beside him. Many of the fireflies were unable to rise, and sank in a long curve like the strands of a weeping willow, but occasionally some climbed high up or flew toward the

137

shore. Young and old on the bridge thronged against the railing on the side facing the tower, and Gimpei walked behind them, looking over their heads. Children hung on the outside of the railing with their nets poised. It seemed incredible that they did not fall off.

As the crowd pressed closer in their struggle to snatch the fireflies, Gimpei wondered at the feeble glimmer of these insects and tried to remember those he had seen on the lake by his mother's village.

"Hey! There's one in your hair!" a man on the bridge called out to a boat under the tower. The girl with the firefly in her hair was unaware that she was being shouted at, and someone else in the boat picked it out.

Gimpei had found her.

She was in a white cotton dress and was looking down at the moat with her arms resting on the railing. Though the rows of people behind her allowed Gimpei only a glimpse of her cheek and shoulders, he knew that he was not mistaken. He took a few steps back, then slowly crept up behind her. The girl's attention was focused on the tower, and there was little chance that she would look round.

She wouldn't have come alone, he thought, but the shock of seeing a boy standing on her left struck him like a knife in the heart. It was a different boy. It was clear even from his back that it was not the same student who had waited for the girl with the dog and had pushed Gimpei down the bank. He was wearing a white shirt, and although he had no cap or coat on, he too seemed to be a student. "Only two months ago," Gimpei thought. Her inconstancy startled him as much as if he had accidentally crushed a flower underfoot. Could her affections really be so fickle compared to his own unwavering devotion to her? After all, though she was with the boy, it didn't necessarily mean they were in love. Yet Gimpei felt that something must have happened between the girl and her other boy-friend. He pushed himself in between the last few people behind the girl and listened, holding onto the railing. More fireflies were being set free.

"I'd like to catch some and take them back to him," she was saying.

"Yes, but fireflies are rather a dismal present for someone who's sick, aren't they?"

"They might be good for him when he can't sleep."

"They're miserable things."

Gimpei realized that the student he had seen two months ago must be ill. As he was afraid the girl might see him if he leaned too far forward, he was forced to watch her profile from a little way behind. Her hair was tied up high in a loop and hung in beautiful, soft waves from the knot. It had been arranged more casually when he had seen her on the slope beneath the ginkgo trees.

139

Though there was little light on the bridge, Gimpei could tell that the boy with her was frailer than the other student. Perhaps they were friends.

"When you next visit him, will you tell him about the firefly-catching?"

"About tonight?..." The student repeated the question to himself. "Mizuno looks happy when I go to see him because we can talk about you. But if I tell him we've been here, he'll probably think there were fireflies flickering all over the place."

"I still want to give him some."

The student didn't answer.

"It's a pity I can't go and see him myself. Do tell him about me, won't you?"

"I always do. He understands, too."

"When your sister took us to see the cherry blossoms that night in Ueno, she said to me 'Machie, you look happy.' But I'm not."

"My sister would be surprised to hear you say that,"

"Why don't you surprise her?"

"Yes." The student laughed casually, but went on as if avoiding the topic, "I haven't seen her myself since then. Wouldn't it be better to let her believe that at least some people are born happy?"

Gimpei, realizing that the boy was also very fond of Machie, had a premonition that she and Mizuno would break up even if Mizuno's health were to improve.

Leaving the railing, he stole up close behind her and stealthily hung the wire handle of the firefly cage onto her belt. The cotton material of her dress seemed heavy, and Machie did not notice him. When he reached the end of the bridge he stopped to look at the cage glowing dimly on her back.

Gimpei wondered what she would do when she discovered the cage hooked onto her belt, and he thought of returning to the middle of the bridge to watch her, hidden by the crowd. After all, it wasn't as if he had slashed the girl's back with a razor blade, so why should he behave like a criminal? Yet he started to walk away from the bridge, aware that Machie had made him discover this timidity in himself, or rather, rediscover it. Convinced by this essay in self-defense, he moved dejectedly toward the ginkgo trees on the slope.

"God! That firefly's huge."

It was a star that Gimpei had seen in the sky, but he instantly mistook it for a firefly, and he said again with deep emotion, "But it's huge. . ."

Rain was beginning to patter on the leaves along the road—large, sporadic drops that sounded like half-melted hail or water dripping from the eaves. It was not the sort of rain one expected in low-lying areas like this, more like the heavy raindrops heard on a night camping out in the hill country beneath tall, broad-leaved trees. Yet the sound was too intense to be taken for a night dew trickling from the leaves. Gimpei had never climbed into the mountains or camped on a plateau, and wondered where he had first heard this strange sound. It must have been by the lake where his mother lived.

"Yet the village isn't exactly on high ground. I've never heard a noise like this before. No. I'm sure I've heard it once. It might be the dying moments of a rainstorm in thick forest, when pools of water on the leaves shed more rain than the sky itself."

"Yayoi-chan, you'll catch cold if you get wet in this rain."

"I wonder if Machie's lover may not have fallen ill after camping out in a rainstorm. Perhaps his bitterness is embodied in this ghostly rain drumming in the ginkgo trees."

Gimpei went on talking to himself in this way, since he liked listening to the sound of the rain when no rain fell.

Tonight Gimpei had learned the girl's name, and reflected that if he or Machie had died the day before, he might never have known it. Then why was he walking away from her up the slope, when this knowledge itself formed some sort of bond between them? But he had already been to the slope twice that evening without knowing what drew him there, and this third visit was inevitable after seeing Machie on the bridge, for the spirit of the girl whom he had left there was under the trees, bearing the cage of fireflies to her sick lover.

It was also a simple urge that had made him hook the cage onto Machie's belt, though in a more sentimental mood he felt that he had hung up his own glowing heart on the girl's body. All he did know was that he had done it secretly, aware that she was anxious to take fireflies to her sick friend.

Ghostly rain fell on the shadow of the girl in white as she floated up the slope beneath the ginkgo trees to see her ailing lover, the cage of fireflies dangling from her belt. . . What a dreadful cliché, Gimpei thought to himself, even for a ghost! Yet though he knew the girl was still with Mizuki by the moat, he couldn't help feeling that her presence was also with him there on the dark slope.

When Gimpei reached the foot of the bank, he tried to climb up it, but got cramp in his leg and clung to the green grass. The grass was slightly damp. His leg did not hurt so much that he had to drag it, but he crawled up on his hands and knees. And as he moved, a baby crawled in the earth beneath him, matching its palms against his as if across a mirror. They were the cold hands of the dead. Bewildered, he remembered a brothel at some hot-spring resort . . . a mirror at the bottom of the bathtub.

When he reached the top of the bank where the student had shouted "You fool!" at him and pushed

143

him down, the day Gimpei had first followed Machie, he stood and watched a streetcar amble along the tracks where the girl had told Mizuno she had seen the red flags of a May Day parade. The light from the windows of the streetcar flickered across the dense, dark trees that lined the street. He continued to gaze intently in its direction, aware that the sound of the phantom rain had ceased.

"You fool!" he shouted suddenly and rolled down the bank, not managing it very well by himself. Just as he was about to hit the asphalt road, he grabbed a handful of grass, pulled himself to his feet and, sniffing his hand, walked along the road, still feeling that the baby was moving with him in the earth of the bank.

He had no idea where his child was, or even whether it was alive or dead. It was one reason why his life had been so uncertain. If it were alive, perhaps he might meet it one day, and he honestly believed he would. But he had no way of knowing whether it was truly his child or someone else's.

One evening, at the entrance to the private boarding-house where Gimpei stayed as a student, a baby had been left with a note saying something like, "This is Gimpei's." The landlady had been upset, but Gimpei had not felt particularly disturbed or ashamed, since one could hardly expect a student to raise an unwanted child—and a prostitute's, what's more—when he

144

might be sent off to the war at any moment.

"It's just a spiteful trick. I left her, and she's done this to get even."

"You ran off when she got pregnant is more like it, isn't it, Mr. Momoi?"

"No, it was nothing like that."

"What were you running away from, then?"

Gimpei didn't answer the question, but said, "Anyway, I'll just take the baby back and have done with it." He looked down at the child lying in the landlady's lap. "Keep it for a while, will you? I'm going to fetch my partner."

"Partner? Partner in what?... Mr. Momoi, you're not going to run off and leave me with this baby, are you?"

"No. It's just that I don't want to take it back by myself."

"What?" The landlady followed Gimpei suspiciously to the door.

When he had found Nishimura, his partner in crime, they set off together, with Gimpei carrying the child, as was only natural since the woman who had abandoned it had been his. He held the baby inside his coat, which he buttoned at the bottom, feeling like a stuffed animal. In the streetcar, the baby inevitably began to cry, but the other passengers smiled in a friendly way at the strange appearance of this university student, and Gimpei returned their smiles, looking embarrassed

145

and faintly comical. He popped the baby's head out of the top of the overcoat, only to realize that he had better keep his own head down, and found himself staring into the child's face.

It was after the great fire in the downtown area of Tokyo caused by the first air raid. Gimpei and his friend set the child down outside the back door of the house and bolted. No one noticed their getaway, since the brothels were not crowded close together in the alley.

Gimpei and Nishimura were old hands at escaping from this house. In those days students were given worn-out, rubber-soled or canvas shoes for their war work, and they often left these shoes behind when they ran out of brothels. They had no money to pay with, but they found the flight exhilarating—like escaping from the shadow of some disgrace. And at work they would wink at each other, saying that their shoes had become too ragged with wear to keep. At least it was fun thinking of places to discard them.

Yet the letters they received from the prostitutes when they ran away were not always demands for money, but often simply invitations to return. The girls knew their names and addresses, since Gimpei and other students like him were destined for the war and had no need to conceal them, for none had any future prospects that would have made such secrecy necessary. Students sent to the front were heroes. But known prostitutes, licensed or otherwise, were usually drafted into the labor force, and Gimpei's woman must have been unlicensed, soliciting in secret. Yet the boys wondered if the brothel system and its regulations hadn't become so lax that an unexpectedly human element had entered into their relations with these women. It never occurred to either of them that the prostitutes might have been afraid of the severe penalties in wartime and forced into this unfamiliar acquiescence. Could they really have sunk so low as to imagine that the women forgave their disappearances as youthful escapades? They had run off three or four times without paying and, as often happened, they had heard nothing since. And when they dumped the baby at the house in the alley, they merely felt that one more final flight had been made.

It was about the middle of March when they went, but it began to snow the following noon and continued until evening. They could not have left the baby to freeze to death in the alley.

Gimpei went out in the snow for a chat with Nishimura in his lodgings.

"We're lucky we went last night, aren't we?"

"Yes, dead lucky."

No one from the brothel had been in touch, and the baby had disappeared.

But had the house in the alley been the same brothel that he had fled from for the last time seven or eight months previously? This nagging doubt occurred to Gimpei after he had been sent to the front. And even if it had been the same brothel, was the child's mother or his woman still there? Could an unlicensed prostitute remain in a brothel once a baby was born, when this was the worst sin of all? It was just possible that in the tense confusion of those days, when an unfamiliar sense of compassion prevailed, a brothel might have cared for a pregnant woman. But it was also most unlikely. And Gimpei thought that it was only when *he* got rid of the baby that it had been truly abandoned.

Nishimura was killed in the war. Gimpei survived and became a schoolteacher, of all professions.

After wandering about the ruins of the area where the brothel had once stood, Gimpei was worn out. All of a sudden he was startled to hear himself say loudly, "Hey! What mischief are you up to now?" He was talking to the prostitute. She had left a child outside the door of his lodgings—not her own child or Gimpei's, but one that she had borrowed from a fellow prostitute. It seemed that he had discovered her at the door, or perhaps run after the woman and caught up with her.

"Nishimura is no longer alive to tell me whether it looked like me or not." He was talking to himself again.

The abandoned baby had been a girl, but strangely enough the sex of the apparition that troubled Gimpei was uncertain. It was usually a dead child, but when he was more normal he felt it was alive.

He thought his little girl had once hit him as hard as she could on the forehead with her plump fist, and when he lowered his head, she had gone on pummeling him. He wondered when it had happened, and decided that it must have been his imagination. Even if the girl were still alive, she would never be as small as he imagined, and nothing like that could ever occur now.

But the ghostly child that moved underground as Gimpei walked along the road below the bank on the firefly-catching night was still a baby, and its sex was indefinite; indeed, it had never been known. And as this thought sank in, the child assumed the monstrous features of a noseless, mouthless dummy.

"It's a girl, a girl," Gimpei muttered to himself as he hurried out into a well-lit street lined with different stores.

"Cigarettes! Give me some cigarettes!" Gimpei called out breathlessly in front of the second store from the corner. An old, gray-haired woman appeared. Though advanced in age, her sex was obvious and Gimpei felt relieved. But Machie seemed infinitely remote, and it required a considerable effort to imagine that a girl like her existed in the world.

He felt his heart unburdened and empty, and for the first time in many days Gimpei remembered his own birthplace. He remembered his beautiful mother, not the father who had died so strangely. Yet his father's ugliness had left a stronger mark on him than his mother's lovely face, just as he was haunted more by the deformity of his own feet than by the beauty of Yayoi's little ones.

By the shore of the lake Yayoi had tried to pick the red berries of a wild *goumi* bush and run a thorn into her little finger. A drop of blood appeared, and Yayoi, sucking the blood and staring at Gimpei with wide, upturned eyes, said: "Gin-chan, why don't you pick the berries for me? Your monkey-feet are just like your father's. I'm sure they don't come from our side of the family."

In a rage Gimpei had wanted to thrust Yayoi's feet into the thorns, but as he didn't dare touch them, he bared his teeth and pretended to bite her wrist.

"Look! You see! That's a monkey-face. Eeee!" Yayoi also showed her teeth.

It was his feet, as ugly as a beast's, that had made the baby follow him, crawling underneath the bank.

Even Gimpei had not tried to examine the feet of the abandoned baby, since he could not seriously believe it was his. In his present mood of masochistic self-disgust, however, he thought that if he had looked at the baby's feet and found them like his own, then it would have provided him with the strongest proof that it was his child. But aren't a baby's feet always soft and lovely before it walks this earth?—like those of the cherubs surrounding the figure of Christ in religious paintings. All feet harden like Gimpei's as they cross the swamps and rocks and thornbushes of this world.

"But if it's a ghost, the child can't have feet," Gimpei murmured to himself. Ghosts don't have legs. He wondered who had first applied this image to ghosts, and thought that there must have been fellow human beings from the earliest times who felt as he did. It was as though his own feet were no longer treading the face of this earth.

Holding out his upturned palm as if to catch gems falling from heaven, Gimpei wandered through the brightly lit streets. It occurred to him that the world's most beautiful mountain is not always some towering, green peak, but a vast, barren mound covered with volcanic ashes and rocks. It is pink and it is purple. It is one with the shifting hues of heaven, at dawn and at sunset. And with this thought, Gimpei decided to turn against that part of him that had longed for Machie.

He remembered the prophetic words that Hisako had spoken as an avowal of either love or separation: "I'll find you—even underground, in the passages below Ueno Station." And, wondering what the passages looked like, Gimpei set off for Ueno.

The place seemed quieter nowadays, and he found only layabouts there now. They seemed to have made it their living-quarters and lay sprawled in the passage or crouched against a wall. It was the usual down-and-out scene: some were stretched out on empty charcoal sacks with baskets beside them; others seemed better off and had large bundles wrapped in cloth behind their heads. All were utterly indifferent to their surroundings and never lifted their eyes to look around or return the stares of passers-by. A number of them had gone to bed enviously early and were already asleep. One young couple had curled up peacefully with the woman resting her head on the man's knees and the man leaning over her back. It would be hard to imitate their contortions even in a night train. They looked like two birds with their heads in each other's feathers, and they were only about thirty. Gimpei stood watching them; a vagrant couple in itself seemed rather unusual.

The dank odor of the subterranean passage mingled with the smell of grilled chicken and Japanese stew. Ducking beneath a shop curtain that seemed to hide nothing but a hollow stone cave, Gimpei had two or three cheap whiskies. A flower-patterned skirt appeared behind his legs, and as he lifted the curtain on his way out he saw a male prostitute standing outside.

The prostitute made eyes at him as they silently exchanged glances. Gimpei took to his heels, but there was no exhilaration in this flight.

He looked inside the upstairs waiting room of the station, but the smell of vagrants filled it too. A station attendant stood at the entrance and asked him for his ticket. It was unusual having to show one's ticket just to get into the waiting room. Other aimless looking people stood around outside or squatted against the wall.

Leaving the station, Gimpei wandered into a backstreet. He was thinking about the double nature of homosexuals when he noticed a woman wearing rubber boots, dressed rather like a man in faded black pants and a filthy white blouse that seemed shrunk from washing. Her breasts were flat, her yellowish face was sunburned, and she wore no makeup. Gimpei glanced round. The woman seemed up to something and, coming closer, began following him. Gimpei, whose experience in chasing women had made him unusually acute in the matter, found himself unable to discover why she was following him.

He remembered the slut who had pestered him—though denying it all the while—when he had sought refuge in a nearby amusement quarter after running away from the iron gate in front of Hisako's house. But from her appearance the present woman was obviously not a prostitute. Her rubber boots were muddy. The mud was not wet, but simply hadn't been cleaned off for days, and the boots themselves were old and discolored. He wondered what sort of woman she could be to walk through Ueno in rubber boots when it wasn't even raining. Was she crippled? Were her legs ugly? Was that why she wore slacks?

Gimpei suddenly thought of his own feet and, imagining the woman's ugly feet behind him, he stopped abruptly to let her pass. The woman also stopped. They stared at each other questioningly.

"What do you want with me?" she said.

"That's what I was going to ask you. You were following me, weren't you?"

"But you looked me over, didn't you?"

"If anybody did, it was you." Gimpei wondered whether he hadn't done something that she might have taken as a signal as he went past, yet he felt certain it was the woman who had shown interest.

"I just glanced at you. I thought your appearance was unusual for a woman."

"I don't think it's particularly unusual."

"Yes, but do you always follow anyone who leers at you a bit?"

"You interested me somehow."

"What's your angle, anyway?"

"Nothing."

"You must have some reason for following me."

"I'm not following you—I'm, well . . . just trying to tag along, that's all."

"I see." Gimpei looked at her again. Her lips were unhealthily dark, without a trace of lipstick, and one

154

gold-capped tooth was showing. It was difficult to say how old she was, but she was probably a little under forty. Her slit eyes were watchful, dry, like a man's, and glinted with cunning; one eye, moreover, was smaller than the other. The skin of her sunburned face was hard. Gimpei sensed a certain danger about her.

"Let's walk on for a bit," he said, abruptly raising his hand to touch her lightly on the breast. There could be no doubt about it. She was a woman.

"What was that you just did?" The woman grasped Gimpei's hand. Her palm was soft. She was obviously not accustomed to rough work.

It was the first time that Gimpei had done this to determine whether a person was a woman. Of course it was quite apparent that she was female, but after making sure with his own hand, Gimpei felt strangely relieved and even friendly.

"Well, let's walk over there," he said.

"Over where?"

"Isn't there some cosy bar we could go to around here?"

Wondering if there was anywhere that he could reasonably take this strangely dressed woman, Gimpei made his way back to the well-lit street. He entered a place where they served Japanese stew, and the woman came in behind him. Seats were arranged along three sides of the square cooking area, and there were separate tables, too.

Since the seats were almost all occupied, he took a table near the entrance. The short curtain above the open door hid all but the lower half of people passing by.

"Saké or beer?" Gimpei asked.

He had no intention of trying anything with this sturdy looking woman, but having found that she wasn't dangerous, he felt relaxed and carefree. He would let her choose whether she wanted beer or saké.

"I'd like saké," the woman answered.

Other simple dishes besides the stew were available, and signs advertising them hung along the wall. Gimpei let the woman order a meal as well. Her familiar manner suggested she might be the kind of woman whose business it was to lure men into some seedy joint or other, but though the description fitted, he preferred not to sound out his theory. Perhaps she had found Gimpei a little frightening and given up the idea of soliciting him, or she might have sensed some common bond between them and decided to follow him. At any rate, she seemed to have abandoned her original purpose for the time being.

"Life's strange, isn't it? I mean, one never knows what'll happen from one day to the next. Here I am drinking with you and I've never seen you before."

"That's right. I've never seen you before," the woman echoed absentmindedly as she downed her drink.

"This day ends with a drink with you, doesn't it?"

"It does, yes."

"Are you going home after here?"

"Yes. I've got a child waiting alone for me."

"A child?"

The woman drank one cup after another. Gimpei spent the time watching her rather than drinking.

He found it hard to believe that in one single night he had seen Machie at the firefly-catching, been pursued by the vision of the baby on the bank, and was now drinking with a woman he had met entirely by chance. Perhaps it was her ugliness that made it possible. To have seen Machie by the moat was a beautiful dream, but this ugly woman in a cheap restaurant was real. Yet drinking with this "reality" seemed at the same time a way to reach the girl in the dream. The uglier the woman, the better the vision. Her ugliness brought Machie's face into view.

"Why are you wearing rubber boots?"

"When I left home, I thought it would rain today."

The woman's answer was explicit. Gimpei felt a desperate urge to see her feet. If they were ugly she would definitely qualify.

The coarseness of her features increased with drink. The narrow, ill-matched eyes grew narrower. With the smaller of the two she gave Gimpei a sidelong glance, swinging her shoulders back and forth. Gimpei grasped her by the shoulders, but she did not stop him.

157

It was like grabbing a handful of bones.

"You shouldn't be so skinny, you know."

"What else do you expect? I'm a single woman with a child to feed."

She told him that she lived with her thirteen-year-old daughter in a rented room in a backstreet and that the child was going to school. Her husband was killed in the war, she said, but though that sounded doubtful, he was satisfied she was telling the truth about the child.

"I'll see you to your room," Gimpei said for the second time.

"No, my place is no good with the child there," the woman replied with sudden decorum, though her first reaction had been to nod in approval.

Gimpei and the woman sat side by side facing the cook, but before he could realize what she was doing, she had turned toward him and was leaning coquettishly against his shoulder. She seemed ready to give herself to him. Gimpei felt overwhelmed with sadness, as though the world were at an end—a sadness out of all proportion to his present circumstances. Perhaps it was because he had seen Machie that same evening.

The way the woman drank was also coarse. Each time she ordered a new bottle of saké she stared up quizzically at him to test his reactions.

"Have another bottle," Gimpei said impatiently.

"I won't be able to walk, you know. Is that all

right?" She put her hand in his lap. "Well, just one more bottle. Pour it in a glass, please."

The saké dribbled from the corner of her mouth onto the table. Her sunburned face had flushed a dark, purplish red.

As they left the place she clung to Gimpei's arm. He held her by the wrist; it was surprisingly smooth.

Passing a girl selling flowers in the street, she said, "Buy some flowers for me, please. I want to take a few home to my child."

But she left the bouquet on the stand of a noodle vendor at a dark streetcorner.

"Keep these for me, will you, friend? I'll be back soon to get them."

Her drunkenness got worse after she left the flowers there.

"I haven't had a man for years, you know. But it can't be helped. I mean, you can't pick and choose, can you?"

"Yes, we're fated for each other," Gimpei reluctantly agreed.

Though he felt nothing but self-loathing as they walked entangled up the street, he still had an urge to see her feet without rubber boots. Yet it seemed he could already see them—toes not simian like his own, but misshapen, with thick, brownish skin. When he pictured himself lying with the woman with their legs stretched out, Gimpei felt like vomiting.

159

For a while he left the woman to lead the way, and entering a backstreet they came in front of a tiny Inari shrine. Next to it stood a cheap hotel where one could spend the night with a girl. The woman hesitated. Gimpei let her clinging arm slide off, and she collapsed in the road.

"If your child is waiting for you, go home," he said and left her.

"You fool! You fool!" the woman yelled and, picking up a handful of small stones in front of the shrine, she began throwing them at him. One of the stones hit Gimpei on the ankle.

"Ouch!" he cried.

He felt miserable as he limped along. Why hadn't he gone straight home after hanging the firefly cage on Machie's back? When he reached his rented upstairs room, Gimpei pulled off his socks. His ankle had turned faintly red.

ACTS OF WORSHIP   Seven Stories

Yukio Mishima / Translated by John Bester

These seven consistently interesting stories, each with its own distinctive atmosphere and mood, are a timely reminder of Mishima the consummate writer.

THE SHŌWA ANTHOLOGY
Modern Japanese Short Stories

Edited by Van C. Gessel / Tomone Matsumoto

These 25 superbly translated short stories offer rare and valuable insights into Japanese literature and society. All written in the Shōwa era (1926-1989).

THE HOUSE OF NIRE

Morio Kita / Translated by Dennis Keene

A comic novel that captures the essence of Japanese society while chronicling the lives of the Nire family and their involvement in the family-run mental hospital.

REQUIEM   A Novel

Shizuko Gō / Translated by Geraldine Harcourt

A best seller in Japanese, this moving requiem for war victims won the Akutagawa Prize and voiced the feelings of a generation of Japanese women.

A CAT, A MAN, AND TWO WOMEN

Jun'ichiro Tanizaki / Translataed by Paul McCarthy

Lightheartedness and comic realism distinguish this wonderful collection—a novella (the title story) and two shorter pieces. The eminent Tanizaki at his best.

CHILD OF FORTUNE   A Novel

Yūko Tsushima / Translated by Geraldine Harcourt

Awarded the Women's Literature Prize, *Child of Fortune* offers a penetrating look at a divorced mother's reluctant struggle against powerful, conformist social pressures.

DISCOVER JAPAN, VOLS. 1 AND 2
Words, Customs, and Concepts

The Japan Culture Institute

Essays and photographs illuminate 200 ideas and customs of Japan.

THE UNFETTERED MIND
Writings of the Zen Master to the Sword Master

Takuan Sōhō / Translated by William Scott Wilson

Philosophy as useful to today's corporate warriors as it was to seventeenth century samurai.

THE JAPANESE THROUGH AMERICAN EYES
Sheila K. Johnson

"Cogent...as skeptical of James Clavell's *Shogun* as it is of William Ouchi's *Theory Z*."—*Publisher's Weekly*

Available only in Japan.

BEYOND NATIONAL BORDERS
Reflections on Japan and the World

Kenichi Ohmae

"[Ohmae is Japan's] only management guru."—*Financial Times*

Available only in Japan.

THE COMPACT CULTURE
The Japanese Tradition of "Smaller is Better"

O-Young Lee / Translated by Robert N. Huey

A long history of skillfully reducing things and concepts to their essentials reveals the essence of the Japanese character and, in part, accounts for Japan's business success.

THE HIDDEN ORDER
Tokyo through the Twentieth Century

Yoshinobu Ashihara

"Mr. Ashihara shows how, without anybody planning it, Japanese architecture has come to express the vitality of Japanese life."
—*Daniel J. Boorstin*

NEIGHBORHOOD TOKYO

Theodore C. Bestor

A glimpse into the everyday lives, commerce, and relationships of some two thousand neighborhood residents living in the heart of Tokyo.

THE BOOK OF TEA

Kazuko Okakura
Foreword and Afterword by Soshitsu Sen XV

A new presentation of the seminal text on the meaning and practice of tea—illustrated with eight historic photographs.

GEISHA, GANGSTER, NEIGHBOR, NUN
Scenes from Japanese Lives

Donald Richie

A collection of highly personal portraits of Japanese men and women—some famous, some obscure—from Mishima and Kawabata to a sushi apprentice and a bar madame.

WOMANSWORD
What Japanese Words Say About Women

Kittredge Cherry

From "cockroach husband" to "daughter-in-a-box"—a mix of provocative and entertaining Japanese words that collectively tell the story of Japanese women.

THE THIRD CENTURY
America's Resurgence in the Asian Era

Joel Kotkin and Yoriko Kishimoto

"Truly powerful public ideas."—*Boston Globe*
Available only in Japan.

THE ANATOMY OF DEPENDENCE
The Key Analysis of Japanese Behavior

Takeo Doi / Translated by John Bester

"Offers profound insights."—*Ezra Vogel*

THE ANATOMY OF SELF
The Individual Versus Society

Takeo Doi / Translated by Mark A. Harbison

"An excellent book."
—*Frank A. Johnson, M.D., University of California, San Francisco*

HOME, SWEET TOKYO
Life in a Weird and Wonderful City

Rick Kennedy

Wry commentaries reveal the charm and humor behind Tokyo's "solemn wackiness."

JAPAN'S LONGEST DAY
The Pacific War Research Society

A detailed account of the day before Japan surrendered.

WORDS IN CONTEXT
A Japanese Perspective on Language and Culture

Takao Suzuki / Translated by Akira Miura

Explores the complex relationship between language and culture.

JAPANESE RELIGION
A Survey by the Agency for Cultural Affairs

Edited by Ichirō Hori

A clear and factual introduction to Japanese Religion.

MIRROR, SWORD, AND JEWEL
The Geometry of Japanese Life

Kurt Singer

"This glimpse of Japanese culture is totally engrossing."
—*Publisher's Weekly*

APPRECIATIONS OF JAPANESE CULTURE

Donald Keene

A glimpse at the complexities that interact to form the Japanese character.
